MILLEWA AND THE AISLE OF FLAMES

BY SOPHIE JOLLY

Dedicated to my Mum who read this first,

To my class of 2022 who cheered me on,

To Brendan for believing that I could.

Chapter One

Beneath the Aisle of Flames

It was Saturday morning when the lands of Apricus woke to the hustle and bustle of the annual Autumn markets, an event that was held in the Wizard Kingdom of Clara on the very first day of Autumn.

From all over, creatures travelled for the prestigious event, trekking far and wide with carts full of goods ready to trade. Everyone had their speciality, a commodity that only their kind could offer.

Wizards brewed and bottled potions for every purpose; curing ailments, one-time power potions and even potions that could make another fall in love with you!

Sprites enjoyed providing delicious delicacies, from lemon butter cake, honeydew sweet tea and lavender crisp biscuits which were always a crowd favourite.

Elves had a handy trade that no one else possessed within the land, which ensured their stalls were always the busiest. They brought along with them exquisite leather bound shoes made from the highest quality skins, their coats were lined with rabbit fur that held a warmth through harsh Winters, each and every article of clothing the Elves brought, always sold immediately to rich wizards whose pockets were never deep enough to hold all their coin.

Although nice to sell to the general wizarding community, it was King Wozil everyone wanted to impress, for anyone who was able to impress the King with their wares, gained special privileges for the remainder of their stay in Clara. Each and every year the quality astounded The King and he was hard pressed picking a winner.

Alma Cornell was nursing her baby whilst the rickety cart stumbled along the cobblestone path towards Clara. Her husband, Fenwick, sat beside her taking in the beauty of his daughter. It had not been easy for Alma to conceive, so they were not disappointed when they were blessed with their baby girl. Fenwick had cherished her from the moment she was born and had not minded that he didn't have a boy to carry his reign of Elven King.

"Was the trip *always* this long, darling?" Alma stifled a yawn, the bumps in the road were quite soothing whilst she fed.

"Oh Alma it isn't much further, we will reach the gates before the sun hits the highest point of the sky," Fenwick didn't mind his wife's impatience when travelling, he had loved her since they were children and was overjoyed when she had agreed to marry him nine years ago.

Fenwick in all his travelling experience wasn't wrong, in fact, the cart came to a gentle halt fifteen minutes prior to noon. The air was crisp and clean, the sun was shining and people were everywhere smiling from ear to ear. The Autumn Market brought the best out in people, it was an event everyone in Apricus could enjoy and take part in.

Clara was enormous, surrounded by tall walls that encapsulated the entire city. High white stone fences that an elf nor a fly could peek through. Pristine hedges provided a luscious skirt to the walls and ivy danced along the stones making it look like a hidden forest.

The buildings within were just as spectacular, light grey castles towered over the wizards below, casting shadows throughout the city.

Flowers blossomed in wooden beds at each wizards' door step, the petal colours changing dependant on the homeowner being present. The streets were lined with cobblestone pavement and neatly trimmed lawns at either side of the path. Streetlamps were dotted on each rounded corner, providing a dim light once The Sun set over the mountainous walls.

A single, circular park resided in the middle of Clara, right in front of King Wozil's gigantic quarters. Its lush green grass and swan shaped fountain provided a natural oasis to the wizards within Clara, with flowers encompassing the perimeter in fierce reds and violent purples, there was no sweeter sanctuary than right here. Or so the wizards believed.

King Wozil's castle stood taller than any other building behind the stone walls. Rich purple tapestry hung from the windows, lined with silver twine and sapphires. His front door consisted of a dark mahogany finish and two large, black door handles that swung open at The King's command. King Wozil's castle was fascinating and daunting all at the same time.

Alma readjusted herself in her seat, sitting straighter and nestling the baby within her arms, hushing her coos. Fenwick smoothed his vest and gently combed his beard with his fingers, trying to be presentable in the presence of The King's land.

"Name, sir?" a short, chubby wizard lifted his eyebrows and looked down his nose towards Fenwick and Alma, hitching up his pants with one hand whilst the other held a list of important townsfolk.

"Fenwick Cornell, King of the Elves and ruler of Dewdrop Springs" Fenwick wasn't offended the wizard did not recognise him, it often happened with 'out-of-towners,' even the important ones like himself.

"Oh of course, sir! Come on in sir, you are most welcome, sir."

The cart sprang to life once more with a lazy wave of Fenwick's hand and it shuffled through the tall, cast iron gate that separated Clara from the rest of Apricus. Inside the gates, Fenwick and Alma are met by another wizard who once again asks for their name. With an excited giggle and blushing red cheeks, the overenthusiastic wizard ushers Fenwick to follow him towards their accommodation for the next two nights. They are led to the large wooden front doors of King Wozil's, with a single knock they swing open with impressive force.

"Welcome, welcome Fenwick, my friend!" King Wozil beamed down at Fenwick who was at least three foot shorter than him. King Wozil was a robust wizard with a large belly and full rosy red cheeks. He dressed only in Alice Blue robes with gold lining and tassels. From head to toe King Wozil asserted himself as the most powerful being in Apricus. Although powerful and dominating, he was also the kindest, ensuring everyone within the lands was fed, happy and always looked after.

"Hello my old friend, I'm so glad we had the chance to meet. You know, with everything going on for the Autumn Market I assumed we wouldn't have the time."

"I will always make time for you, Fenwick. But for now, we must see you to your chambers and after, we sweep the markets for the finest wares. Tomorrow we shall discuss the unrest in Apricus." Wozil smiled solemnly, they had been peaceful for such a long time.

Down the hall, on the last left was Fenwick and Alma's room. It was as extravagant as Alma had expected and remembered from previous trips. Oak floors that were laden with swirls and grooves, cut from the tallest trees in the valley. The walls were a simple beige, oak trims and a huge window that overlooked the park below. It was beautifully lit with at least two dozen thick candles and an enormous gold chandelier that hung from the ceiling like a crown bejewelled by light.

Alma felt completely out of place whenever they visited, even more so now they had a baby. A gold studded cot sat beside their four poster bed and Alma sighed at the magnificence of it all. Being a queen of a town was not how she imagined her life, smiling and waving at important events, curtseying at dinners to people she had never met and ensuring she was always well groomed.

Alma Cornell was not equipped to be such a lady.

The afternoon was balmy when the market stalls were being set up, the sky a mixture of burnt orange and soft pink hues. The sun grazed the backs of the shop owners, sweat beginning to drip down their brows.

It was unusually warm for the first of March when the markets take place, usually the afternoons were cold and uninviting, but there was heat to the wind and people were everywhere. Rows and rows of stalls were set up along the curved streets.

Ribbons hung from their frames with large signs written in cursive, eluding to the wares strewn across the wooden tables. Fenwick and Alma had never seen a busier market. They shuffled through the crowds, peeking at the cakes and sweet teas the Sprites had on offer.

"How much for your jam, custard and scones may I ask?" Alma's mouth was watering at all the delectable options. Though small, the Sprites were excellent cooks and always sourced the most interesting flavours.

"For you Queen Cornell, it shall be two gold dollars and three silver cents, which flavours do you desire madam?" The Sprite serving Alma was sweet, no older than twelve and wore bright green with a matching bow.

"I will take three of your blueberry beetle jam jars, two of your thick rhubarb custard tins and at least a dozen tea tree scones, they are most certainly my favourite."

Fenwick pondered the main street, shuffling his feet as he walked. He hitched his cream linen pants up higher to let the breeze cool his legs.

His mind was heavy and clouded, he was struggling to enjoy the calming afternoon. Just as he reached the Elven shops to greet his people, someone slipped beside him and whispered in his ear.

"I do not mean to alarm you, but there will be an urgent meeting in King Wozil's chambers. Now. Please don't delay." A tall, grey wizard was standing behind Fenwick. Finfudune Bosmerch, King Wozil's advisor. A quiet wizard who often whispered in Wozil's ear during important meetings.

Fenwick didn't completely trust Finfudune, but knew better than to stir trouble where it wasn't necessary.

"Bosmerch? Whatever is the matter?" Fenwick turned to see

he had disappeared with a swish of his robes.

Before he even made the front doors of King Wozil's castle, a ring of fire appeared around the walls of Clara. Hot, monstrous flames engulfed the ivy and gates, like flaming snakes constricting the outer wall. Blackened ash fell from the sky, blinding everyone who dared look up. The doors to the castle were sealed shut, impossible to move by hand. Fenwick motioned his hands in a circle and with impressive force, the door blew open to the hallway inside.

Fenwick shut the doors behind him, it was eerily quiet inside, not a mouse nor a wizard could be heard through the thick concrete that encased him.

He turned to his right, the door to Wozil's office was shut. CRASH, BANG! The sound of glass shattering and a window being broken from inside.

Fenwick slowly opened the door handle when he was bowled over by a figure much larger than himself.

The window was smashed, leaving with it a hole the size of a horse.

"Fenwick, oh thank goodness, Fenwick! King Wozil is dead. The orcs have gone mad, save your loved ones, save your child. They killed Wozil and are killing babies as sport. Please hurry, we don't have much time." Finfudune looked manic, his once straight, grey hair was sticking up on end and his long beard that was usually tied in a neat knot was frayed. His wild eyes searched for an answer within Fenwick's kind face and found that he knew as little as him right in this moment.

Without hesitation Fenwick ran as fast as his little legs would take him, fiercely searching for his wife and child. After ten minutes of pushing through crowds of the panicked, injured and dead, Fenwick found Alma huddled under a broken stall, gripping her baby so tightly it was a wonder she could breathe.

"Alma, it isn't safe anymore. Wozil has been murdered by the orcs and they are searching for children to slay. We need to get her out of here, wherever we can, as far as possible, we can't let her die." Alma's face was in shock, her mouth lay open, her bright eyes now pale and soullessly staring at her husband. "Alma, please. We need to hurry, I need to try stop this, but not until I know our daughter will be safe."

Alma stood slowly and unravelled the baby from her chest, her small hands still gripping her mother's shirt.

"If you insist, I will make her safe. It is not easy, but it is for the best" Alma kissed her child and placed her small frame on the cobblestone path. She methodically began to swish her arms in long, controlled strokes, her eyes closed and concentrated. After her seventh round, a ring of pearly white appeared directly in front of her. Its wispy figure angelic against the harsh backdrop of a burning city. She held her hands firmly in place, concentrating only on the ring.

"Pick her up, Fenwick. And throw her in." Alma did not flinch and did not stammer. Fenwick obeyed his wife's orders and tossed his baby girl through the portal. "With all my love you may live, Millewa."

The white ring vanished and the city of Clara was buried in flames.

Chapter Two

The Odd One Out

Millewa strained to open her eyes. She could hear her siblings shouting down stairs, crashing into furniture and playing loudly. This was a regular occurrence in her household. Millewa's foster parents had recently taken in twins, totalling the children living there to an even six.

She rolled in her bed and stretched her limbs, even though she was sixteen years old, she still fit snuggly in her single bed, wrapped in her fluffy green doona. She looked around her room, the walls littered with posters from magazines, her favourite artists taking up the most space.

Books piled high along the wall, the ones she'd got as presents but never yet bothered to read, mixed in with her countless scrapbooks that she'd attempted to start but not finished.

She gave a loud yawn and stretched again, feeling every ounce of her body release and relax. Millewa peered towards her window, the light peeking through edges, willing her to get up and start the day. She closed her eyes once more when her bedroom door creaked and a voice whispered from the crack.

"Morning sleepy head, how are you feeling? It's still quite early if you want to stay in bed." Millewa's foster Mum, Stella, was the kindest soul she knew. She doesn't know where she'd be without her or how she could possibly face each day.

Millewa was found on the edge of town, wrapped in singed blankets with ash and dirt covered cheeks and a note that read: *My name is Millewa*. Her case was a mystery to police and how she came to be where she was, with no connection to anyone, from there, she entered the foster system.

After two years of being bounced from family to family, Millewa fell into the laps of Stella and John. They have loved her immensely from the moment they picked her up from the foster care office, her tiny frame, her striking blue eyes with a hint of yellow and her infectious laugh that could make anyone smile.

Stella and John were shocked when they heard how Millewa was found as a baby and wondered what awful people could have just dumped her in a disgusting area in filthy clothes. They vowed that when they took her in they wanted to give her the most amazing life possible, one that she could remember, not like her questionable early year.

Stella and John had only ever fostered, not being able to have children of their own. Little did Millewa know, they were in the process of trying to adopt her.

The house was always chaos. A large double story home in the suburbs with a grassy backyard that was always covered in trucks and toys. A red tiled roof and green painted weatherboards, the house looked like Santa Clause had thrown up on it, not to mention the three-year-old Christmas decorations that clung to the gutters desperately, John had never bothered to take them down even though they were broken.

The windows were always open and fresh air flooded the house along with a stream of light that warmed the bedrooms. Inside the house the floors were dark and always dusty, with light walls and wooden accents, it had a homely feel that was always welcoming. The whole house was built around the kitchen and the family spent most of their time together cooking, cleaning or having musical concerts with the cooking utensils. It may not have been the biggest or the best, but Millewa loved it all the same, it was comforting to finally have a place she could call home. Even if sometimes it didn't feel so inviting.

"Move OVER! Just move! You are always getting in my way which makes *zero* sense since you're like two foot tall." Drew pushed Millewa out of the way in the line for breakfast.

"I am NOT two foot tall. I'm three and a quarter feet." Millewa had this argument weekly with Drew and Ellie, both whom were two years older than her and constantly making fun of her appearance. It was no secret to any of the kids that Millewa was their parents' favourite, they believed that because she was so abnormal, that *must* be why they favoured her. Millewa got her own room, the one in the house with the big windows and tall ceilings, she also got the softest and comfiest bed of them all, that had pillows as cosy as clouds. She got to paint her room whatever colour she wanted and always got the best toys at Christmas. Millewa's siblings despised her and continually grew jealous of her prejudice.

"Whatever. You still are the most annoying thing I have ever met. I say thing because there is *no way* you could possibly be human. I mean, *look at you.*" Ellie knew she had hit a nerve, smirking at the look on Millewa's face. Millewa's eyes became glassy and tears began streaming down her face. Her siblings weren't the only ones to pick on her.

At school, Millewa was subjected to regular ridicule and tormenting from her peers and she often found herself eating her lunch out of bounds behind the library building. She was short in stature with gently defined features. Her eyes were big and blue, like looking deep into the depths of the ocean. Her hair was thick blonde and cut short just above her thin shoulders.

She was teased for her clothing, as she only fit into toddlers' clothes and all the prints were made for babies. Aside from her miniscule frame, Millewa had small ears that instead of rounding at the top, were pointed. After regular doctors' appointments, they had discovered that there was nothing dangerously different about Millewa, she was just born with oddities.

Without knowing her parental background, there was no way of telling if there was anything seriously wrong with her.

It was the final day of school before the Spring school holidays and Millewa could not be more excited. Spring holidays meant exploring the local forests, swimming in the lake and sunning yourself on the banks of the river. Millewa always felt so relaxed in nature and found herself continually gravitating outside no matter what the weather.

The bus pulled up on the corner of their road. Stella had the kids there ready and waiting five minutes prior, as usual to ensure they weren't late for school.

"Have a lovely day my darlings! Lunch is packed and your water bottles are full. Please be kind to one another." Stella was well aware that Millewa wasn't liked by her siblings and that their hatred of her projected on to her school peers, meaning she had no friends. Stella kissed each one of their heads as they piled onto the school bus, she didn't stop waving until they turned the corner. She then took a huge sigh and turned to walk back to the house.

Millewa sat at the front of the bus, eyes forward and ignoring the taunts that were launched at her from behind. She chose to ignore them as best she could, not wanting to cause more trouble than necessary, that's when the slurs about her ears were thrown around: *obviously the points make it hard to hear* or *she's deaf and ugly.* These were just a few choice phrases that struck Millewa like a lightning bolt. The bus ride was always tense and Millewa sat with her bag on her lap to hide her legs anxiously bouncing up and down. Halfway to school, a girl in primary school gets on and sits next to her. It was comforting to have Remy there for the majority of the trip, she didn't talk much but she also didn't insult Millewa which is all she could ask for.

"Do you know why your ears are so pointy?" Remy stared at Millewa with her glasses low over her nose, her long fringe poking in her eyes.

"No, the doctors said there was nothing wrong and I must've just been born that way." Millewa shrugged and was taken aback by Remy's sudden interest in her appearance.

"Hm. I think you're magical then. It can be the only explanation. You're like a shimmering fairy." Remy's eyes sparkled and she stared right into Millewa's eyes. Millewa had never thought of herself as magical before, she appreciated Remy and her immaturity, her inquisitiveness and wonder is what made Millewa feel different that day. She wasn't a weirdo or a freak. She was magic.

The abuse didn't contain itself to the bus, in fact, within the classrooms it was ten times worse. Millewa always tried to sit herself at the back, so she couldn't feel everyone's eyes glaring at her or hear the whispers that erupted as soon as the teacher turned her back. This didn't always help, because more often than not, the other students had no shame in turning their chairs to stare and point.

There was only so much she could take before she'd call to the teacher to use the bathroom, where she'd sit in the stalls and cry until the bell rang for her next lesson.

Recess and lunch were challenging, more so in the fact she was running out of places to hide. The regular bullies kept finding her in heating vents, under play equipment and even in trash bins when she got really desperate. When they did find her, there was nothing she could do to escape, she wasn't fast enough to outrun them or strong enough to fight back. That is when she would spend the rest of her break, hanging upside down from the monkey bars, tied up with students' shoelaces, she would be ridiculed and laughed at for her appearance. She'd call to her older siblings, hoping they may get her down but alas they would turn the other way and pretend they did not hear her.

As much as the teachers tried to control this, there was no stopping the inevitable wrath Millewa faced almost daily. To say she was excited for the last day of term was an understatement.

School finished an hour early that day, to allow the teachers some time to pack up and relax on the final day of the term. None of the students complained and skipped their way out of the gates towards the bus lines. Stella stood nearby, ice creams in hand and a massive grin on her face.

"We're going on a holiday! Surprise!" All the kids looked at her with amazement, their confused faces broke into large smiles that split across their round faces. Having six children and a low income meant the family never got away for more than one night, the word 'holiday' was special for each and every one of them.

Stella and John had been saving their pennies for a while and finally scrounged enough to take the kids away for four nights to the Silvan National Park.

The park resided two hours away from the family home in the foothills of the Ingens Mountains, but where they were staying was at least another hour from the park entry. They had rented a wooden cabin on a big reserve near the Crus Lake, there were paddle boats and canoes for the kids to use and a BBQ pit right outside their front door.

It was always hard travelling so far away with children, especially now they needed a ten seater van to squeeze them all in. Stella and John had learned to manage and make the best of everything they could.

After a long three terms of school, they all deserved a break.

Chapter Three

Ingens Mountain

John burst into Millewa's room, the sun hadn't even risen for the day. He flicked on her light and opened her curtains, as if that would provide any additional light. The brightness was harsh on her eyes and she rubbed them gently to try stifle the fluorescence.

John couldn't contain his excitement to finally take the family away. The weather forecast was clear skies, sunny and warm, everything they could've hoped for. They knew nothing was going to rain on their parade.

"Get packing kiddo, I want to leave within the hour. I've got a big breakfast waiting downstairs once you're ready." John tussled Millewa's short hair and skipped through her doorway, leaving it wide open. Drew stumbled past with a toothbrush in his mouth, using one hand to carry his luggage and the other to smooth down his dark curls.

"What are you looking at warthog?" Millewa grimaced as toothpaste flew out of Drew's mouth onto her carpet.

"I'm just wondering how someone as *clever* as you still manages to look so *stupid* all the time." Millewa had approximately three seconds to move before Drew launched his sticky toothbrush at her, foam pouring from his mouth and splattering her belongings as he yelled profanities at her. Millewa slammed the door in his face and locked it, that was the best birthday present she had ever asked for, a lock on her door.

Millewa pulled out her navy blue sports bag and started piling her belongings into it. Her toothbrush, socks, undies, shorts and four different t-shirts. She didn't like taking too much away with her and would much rather have a light bag than hurt her back trying to carry half her bedroom.

She turned off her light and made her way down the stairs to the kitchen.

A delectable smell of bacon and toast filled the air. Plates of scrambled and fried eggs, grilled tomatoes and thick sausages were lined up along the island bench. A stack of eight plates waited on the edge to be filled. A jug of orange juice and apple juice were placed on the table with glasses of ice, if there was one thing John knew how to do, it was breakfast.

"This smells *amazing,* Dad." Jessie's mouth was watering and she bounced on her feet, too excited to wait. John was giving the sausages a final turn before scooping them onto the plate.

After that, it was carnage. The six kids all pushed and shoved one another, trying to be the first in line to fill their bellies. Jessie shoved Drew, Drew pulled Ellie's hair, Jasper bit Jessie and

Cassie fell face first into the eggs. If there was one thing Stella and John's kids knew how to do, it was to completely destroy a nice family meal.

Stella rolled her eyes and gently started lining the kids up, in height order. Despite being one of the eldest, Millewa was pushed right to the back behind the twins. Stella kissed Millewa on the head and passed her a plate. Millewa knew it wasn't personal and didn't mind needing to stand behind everyone.

After breakfast, Stella loaded the dishes into the dishwasher, leaving a few in the sink to soak. John started picking up the luggage with a heave and taking it towards the car.

"You kids pack more and more every time we go away; you can't possibly have that much stuff." John groaned as he picked up Ellie's bag, she always had to take her full case of makeup with her, especially if they were going to be gone for four whole days.

The twins had filled their bags with soft toys and remote control cars, requiring them to be repacked by Stella so they actually had clothes to take away.

Drew tried to smuggle his PlayStation and Cassie panicked and packed her whole bookcase.

John and Stella exchanged a look of hopelessness when they realised they shouldn't have relied on six kids to pack without supervision. John shut the car boot, piled the children in and buckled his belt. They were finally ready to go, two and a half hours since he'd woken everyone up.

The sun was blazing through the windscreen; John had sweat developing on his thick brow as he cranked the cars air conditioning system. Everyone in the car kept shuffling themselves uncomfortably from the heat, unsticking their legs from the leather seats.

They were nearly two hours into their trip, finally reaching the edge of the Ingens Mountain Region where they stopped for lunch. Stella had prepared ten ham and cheese sandwiches on fresh, buttered white bread, knowing that at least two of her children would want seconds. She packed juice boxes in varying flavours and a pack of cold water bottles which were stored in the esky.

John steered the car into a rest area nearby, trees as tall as towers loomed over the benches, providing much needed shade from the blistering sun. They all piled out of the car, looking for some relief from the stifling heat, instead they were met with a wall of steaming air that choked their lungs.

Stella handed out the sandwiches, ensuring each child at least had one, then she gave a round of juice boxes. Sandwiches were gobbled and juices inhaled, they were all after one thing only: a swim in the nearby river.

Before Stella and John could get their swimmers on, the kids were racing down to the water diving and bombing into the cool, blue waterway.

Millewa ambled down to the water's edge, staring at her hot and sweaty reflection. She splashed her face and trickled water down her arms. A cool breeze had picked up and tickled the water on her body. She laid back on the bank and closed her eyes, taking in the sounds of nature around her; birds chirping, wind rustling leaves and the steady flow of the stream.

"How much longer will we be here for Mum?" Millewa hadn't yet opened her eyes, relaxing every inch of her tiny frame.

"I think at least another hour, it's too hot in that car and the water is so lovely. We could even just camp here!" Stella floated on her back in the shallows, letting the gentle current take her before swimming back slightly and repeating the process.

"As much as I would *love* to camp here, it isn't allowed" John pointed to a sign that had a big, red cross through a tent "Also, we've paid for accommodation at the 'Silvan Lodge,' I wouldn't want to waste that."

"Do I have time for a small hike then, Dad? I promise I won't go far; I just want to see the area before we go."

"As long as you are super-duper careful and don't get lost, I don't want to be out there in the dark looking for you." John had Drew by the ankle, attempting to hold him back from dunking his sister.

"I promise; I'll make sure I stick to the stream." Millewa picked up her water bottle and started on the narrow track alongside the riverbed.

It didn't take long for Millewa to begin sweating, the sun beat down on her shoulders and back, wetting her singlet and shorts. She stopped by the water and dipped her socks and runners in, trying to keep her feet cool.

This part of the forest was incredible, Millewa couldn't believe they lived only two hours from here, it felt like a different world.

She continued to walk and take in the beauty of the nature around her. The track beneath her feet had almost completely disappeared and was replaced by greeny brown leaves and moss covered rocks. The trees loomed over her, creating a continual shadow and giving her a rest from the intense heat. Trees of all shades of green surrounded her, their dark trunks merging into a sea of grainy brown.

She immersed herself in the quietness of her surroundings and marvelled at finally having some alone time from her relentless siblings.

After about thirty minutes of trekking, Millewa started to wonder if she would be able to find her way back, although she'd stuck to the river, she was now unsure which way was 'back.'

She slipped on the slick path, bouncing off a rock as she landed heavily with a thud. The surrounds of brown and green became dizzying, Millewa realised with unrelenting anxiousness that she was in fact, lost.

How could she get lost? She strictly followed her father's

instructions and stuck to the trail directly adjacent to the stream, ensuring she didn't go too far off the beaten track.

Although the trees provided much needed shade, Millewa became hot and began to sweat profusely. How would she find her way back? What if her family left without her? She was certain that Drew would be overcome with joy at the thought of Millewa being lost forever. Millewa stood up and began to brush the dirt off her sticky legs, she adjusted her cap and attempted to listen for any sign of her family's direction. Nothing.

"Mum! Dad! Can you hear me?!" Millewa's calls were met with more silence, all she could hear was the soft trickle of the water, buzzing bees and…

"Psst"

"Very funny Drew. I'm glad you found me though, I was beginning to think I'd wandered too far." Millewa turned herself in the direction of the whisper, assuming she would be staring straight at her older brother.

When Millewa turned towards the mass of trees however, she saw nothing. Nothing but more of the same dark trunks and luscious leaves that had accompanied her the last hour. She turned on her heel again towards the water and started to her left.

"Pssssst" There it was again, as clear as before, a whispering call to Millewa. It couldn't have been to anyone else because as far as she knew, she was the only one within that radius. Millewa's confidence began to wane and she stammered towards the trees, her knees wobbling and knocking as she moved towards the sound.

“H – Hello?” Sweat dripped down her brow, her hands shaking uncontrollably. Was this where she met her end? What if the stories Drew told her about the crazy axe murderer in the National Park were true?

Millewa straightened herself and took a deep breath. Clutching her pack, she noticed an extravagant bush, the brightest green she had seen all day, dotted with vibrant yellow flowers. Curious, she hadn’t yet spotted any flowers on her hike. She leant towards the bush, pressing her ear against the budding blooms.

“Hello Millewa” with a fright she stumbled backwards, regaining her position she leant forwards once more. Through the break in the branches she could see a young face, no younger than herself but no older. A huge grin split across his thin face, his yellow eyes bulging with delight.

“I have been waiting for you to hit this part of the track *all* day. It took you long enough to get here! The name’s Sydare, Sydare Jones.” Millewa gaped at what stood in front of her.

Sydare was small, like her, his eyes were as spritely as daffodils and his dark hair was tousled across his face in long, tight curls. He had long fingers and feet, that bore no shoes or gloves. He wore pants of cream linen and a blue, loose fitting collared shirt.

Millewa was perplexed, although she looked different to him

and they had never met, Sydare had a familiarity about him that she couldn't shake.

She studied his features and clothes intensely, not saying a word to him whilst her eyes scanned every detail, landing at his ears. His ears that were not too large or too small, but ears that did meet in a crisp point at the top. Exactly like her own.

"How do you know who I am? I can't possibly have met you before, I think I would've remembered" Millewa stood assertively, as if she were on guard, not wanting to give too much away.

"We have met, briefly, a long time ago. I don't expect you to remember, I don't even remember the moment myself, but my dad explained to me in great detail how important you are. I'm so grateful to have found you, this will mean so much to the people of Apricus. We must get going though, the Sun will set soon, it will be much nicer for you to walk there in the light of day." Sydare outstretched his hand to grasp Millewa's.

She stood there with a puzzling look, not understanding what on Earth this boy meant.

"I – I – I have no idea what you want or need from me, or even where you are from, but I cannot help you and I must be getting back to my family. It was nice to meet you, Sydare."

"Oh dear Millewa, you and I are of the same kind, can't you see? I know you are intrigued and so you should be. It's not every day you learn you're not human" Sydare began to laugh.

"You also must not understand that my invitation is not for decline, in fact it is quite the opposite." With a flick of his wrist and muttering breath, Millewa was bound at the ankles and wrists. An eye mask placed over her head, blacking out everything around her.

Millewa felt cold as she was led to the unknown, the smooth mossy path now gone as her shoes began to crunch crisp leaves and sticks that lay beneath her feet.

Chapter Four

Dewdrop Springs

The trickling of the river and chirping of birds was soon mute, a deafening silence surrounded Millewa whilst she walked slowly to an almost menacing beat. All she could hear was the clank of her chains and her increased breath as she anxiously walked with Sydare.

Every so often, he would loudly whistle or hum a mysterious tune, as if trying to signal other parties they were near. Millewa did not make a sound or try to engage in conversation, the less she knew, the better, she thought.

After what seemed like hours of trudging through the thick forest, spindly branches whipping her in the face and fuzzy leaves tickling her nose, they came to an abrupt halt. Without warning, Millewa's blindfold disappeared and the light blinded her sparkling blue eyes, wincing as she struggled to adjust her focus.

Sydare carefully unchained her wrists and ankles, studying her face intently, as if trying to gauge whether she would run if he let her go. Where on Earth would she run to? She was surrounded by tall oak trees that thrust into the air like skyscrapers, their trunks as thick as trucks, the roots tangling and dancing with each other obstructing the dusty path. Their leaves casting a canopy over the forest floor, keeping them cool whilst pockets of sun fought to touch their toes. Millewa had never felt smaller in her life.

She took in her surroundings, trying to identify every leaf and every groove in the trees, trying to find something that would elude to where she was. Alas, after her continual gazing, everything began to look the same.

"Sydare… where are we? The forest is different here, more serene, more, beautiful" Millewa couldn't quite put her finger on it, but here, she felt calm.

"Welcome Millewa, home, to Dewdrop Springs" a wide grin spread across Sydare's thin face, his eyes now kind and warm. He outstretched his hand to Millewa, she grabbed it eagerly. For the first time all day she felt her heart race with excitement, she had been captured, chained and led to an unknown land, by someone who looked wildly similar to her, it was more than a coincidence their paths crossed.

With his left hand holding Millewa's right, Sydare used his right pinky finger to trace a pattern along the thickest tree trunk, an intricate work of art that glowed yellow after every stroke. Sydare stepped back, the tree was illuminated in gold, swirls and edges carved deep into the trunk. The middle of the masterpiece was what looked like a portrait of Sydare himself, his pointed ears and long hair distinctive amongst the detail. Sydare turned to Millewa, still tightly gripping her hand.

"Are you ready?" No sooner the words had left his lips the tree began to crack. The ground beneath them shaking fiercely. Each detail began to fade and the tree receded and folded against itself, creating a giant wooden archway tangled in vines and roots, the words 'Dewdrop Springs' carved high into the arches.

Millewa gaped at the magic that appeared right in front of them, the sheer enormity of the entrance was enough to make anyone's jaw drop. The path was cleared and golden dust paved the way, oak trees surrounded them as they took their first steps through the passage, a tunnel of bright green trees encasing them in cool darkness. Sydare strode confidently through, leaving Millewa to trail behind, the path bending as they went.

As they walked, the trail began to widen, the bushy thicket of trees lessening with each step, the light escaping every slit. Before she knew it, Millewa was standing on the edge of a grand clearing.

A huge fountain sat in the middle of the area, a stout man carved from stone perched atop the structure, whilst bright blue water cascaded from its many jets into the pool below. Hugging the edges of the clearing were Giant Redwood trees, each with carvings and holes etched into its trunk, with spurts of light escaping tiny windows and doors. Pulley systems attached at their base with baskets that could hold up to five people. Each branch coiled with that of the next tree, what looked like small houses were perched on these bridgings and figures could be seen walking between.

Millewa strained her eyes, trying to take in every ounce of what she was seeing, a completely new world in which she had stumbled, one of treehouses and magic.

"This is incredible! You live here?!" Millewa rounded on Sydare, her eyes glistening in the afternoon sun.

"I certainly do, you once did too, before, you know, you went away" Sydare looked sheepish and shy, he hadn't been sure how to raise this with Millewa, the fact he knew her previously and that he needed her help. He had searched for years to find her, now standing in front of him, his search was complete.

"What do you mean *used* to live here? I was found at the edge of Blackmount, no trace of where I had come from. How do you know me?"

"I… Um… Are you hungry? It's been a long day and we've had barely anything to eat! Quick come this way I'll show you the bakery," Sydare grabbed Millewa's arm and dragged her towards the fountain, darting left along the pathway towards the other side of trees.

The trees were still mountainous, but Millewa couldn't see nearly as many light filled windows as the main square. Instead, the bases were lined with what appeared to be shops, butted together tightly all with unique fronts, inviting shoppers to enter.

They seemed to have everything you'd ever need, a grocer filled with fresh fruits and vegetables whose shop front had shrubs that self-harvested and another whose fruit was ready within minutes. There was a tailor that measured you as you walked through the door, a seed market filled with exotic seeds from all around the lands. Millewa picked up an orange packet of seeds that instantly burnt her hands, leaving red raw welts and blisters.

"Firefly plant. Only Sprites can handle the heat, they use it only for medicinal purposes. Here, come this way, we'll get that hand sorted." Sydare showed Millewa to the next shop.

"What's a Sprite?" Millewa caressed her hand as she followed Sydare slowly.

"A Sprite is one of the many creatures of our world. They are small, *deadly* clever and are the menders of our world, meaning any ailments you may have, they can mend you."

"Creatures? What world is this?" Sydare pretended not to hear her and continued leading her towards the next strip of shops.

A large windowed shopfront stood towering over the rest, a large green cross protruding from its roof. Three fairy like creatures stood out the front with pieces of bark, madly scribbling with long quills as they were told of symptoms. Each were draped in bright periwinkle feathers with thickly knitted skirts that were jagged at the edge. Their hair was long and plaited intricately with ribbons and leaves folded through the creases and large translucent wings that sparkled in the sunshine, the veins matching their clothing. They had human features, with pointed noses and sharp bone structure, lanky legs and arms, they were tiny humans with magical properties.

Millewa thought they were beautiful, glowing humanoids that could heal with a click of their fingers.

Millewa and Sydare joined the line behind another Sprite, this one was eloquently dressed in vibrant greens and red, with a large boil jutting from their neck.

"What seems to be the matter?" the Sprite in periwinkle asked.

"Well, I was gardening in the wizard garden, picking strawberries and dew grass as I always do. Out of nowhere this earwig *bit* me right on the neck. It wasn't one of those regular ones, but a sickly yellow colour" the green Sprite suddenly looked very pale, as if he may be sick.

"Very well, Mender Marsh is best suited to insect injuries, he's got quite a wait if you don't mind" the nursing Sprite was furiously recording the information on her bark. "*Next.*"

Millewa stepped forward tentatively.

"What's the matter?" this Sprite was extremely stern and had obviously been doing this job for a long time.

"I... My hand" Millewa stretched her hand out, the blisters were filled with pus and were split all across her palm.

"Oh my dear, are you daft? Firefly plants cannot be handled by your kind, don't you know that?" her face was now relaxed and kind, almost pitying Millewa's supposed stupidity. "Mender Shaw will see you shortly, she hasn't got a long wait."

Mender Shaw sprinkled icy dust over Millewa's hand and bandaged it with ferns to keep it cool. The experience befuddled her and how easily and quickly her blisters became new skin, then it was as if the incident had never happened.

They continued their dawdling, Millewa gawking at the shops she hadn't recognised the first time. They passed the flower shop with everlasting varieties, the candy shop that had the oddest flavours imaginable. Lemon and grass seed chocolate bars, lavender myrtle bubble gum (which can blow bubbles to the size of cars), honey covered ants and spicy candied petunias. Sydare bought Millewa a dewdrop lollipop, famously made in the freshwater spring nearby.

A wing repairer stood alone, giant cascading wings beat down a heavy draft from its ceiling, large oak doors leading within. It was like a dream. One thing the shops all had in common, Millewa realised, was the name 'Jones' appeared on almost all of the signage. Whoever owned all this, Millewa thought, must have been extremely wealthy.

"Jones… Jones… Where I have heard that name before…" Millewa thought aloud, scouring the overhead signs. Sydare smiled gingerly.

"Ah yes, well. My uh, family, own Dewdrop Springs. We bought it when it when the town collapsed after… Actually you don't need to know that." Sydare said it with such finality,

Millewa thought it best to not ask any more questions.

The Sun began to set over the clearing, a cool breeze tickling Millewa's nose. Her stomach rumbled loudly like a train, she realised she hadn't eaten any proper food today.

"You must be hungry, I'm sorry I'm a terrible host. Let's go home and have dinner" with a flash Sydare started again, walking briskly in the opposite direction to which they came.

The main square had many paths leading off it, Millewa assumed they twisted off to more towering Redwoods and tree homes.

Just on the other side of the clearing, Sydare took a narrow walkway that lead to one, huge tree that stood alone and away from all the others. A pine gate separated them from the tree and Sydare clicked it open with his hands. The garden was immaculately kept, rows and rows of berry bushes lined the front yard, a pebbled path led to the base of the tree where a single red door was cut into the middle. Passionfruit vines tangled themselves around the low-lying branches and a small pond lay just East of the luscious vegetable patch.

"Yep," Sydare stared shyly, "this is home." Sydare opened the door and ushered Millewa inside, a circular staircase wrapped around the inside of the wide trunk, Millewa dizzied herself trying to trace it all the way to the top.

She gave a sigh of relief when Sydare pulled a lever that dropped the pulley system down. They hopped inside and began the journey towards the living quarters, placed in the top end of the tree.

The smell of braised meat and vegetables filled the air as they neared the peak. With a slight jolt the pulley stopped and the gate opened towards a large entry, glowing with warm light. Millewa looked above the doorway. Wooden letters nailed in solidly, presenting the name 'Jones.'

"Hey Mum, Dad! We've got an extra guest who will stay with us for a little while" Sydare grabbed Millewa's hand and moved into the living area.

The main room was split into three areas, a cosy living room with a roaring open fire that cast light to every corner. Two squishy couches were draped in woollen blankets, a woven rug strewn across the hardwood floor. A dining room sat adjacent, a solid dining table and chairs filled the area. Large goblets and golden cutlery and crockery laid across the leafy placemats, a steaming pot in the middle of the table with a crackling flame beneath its base. Homemade artworks and pictures papered the walls, reminding Millewa of her own home. Oil lamps were dotted about and the large windows were cloaked in heavy material to keep out the cold. Straight ahead of the entry was the kitchen, an enormous bench, parallel to them was covered in food scraps, cooking utensils and pans. Pots hanging from the ceiling, oak cupboards full of crockery in every metal and a sizeable fire pit where pots and pans were bubbling and splattering away.

The smell was incredible, freshly baked bread and wattleseed, toasted nuts and seeds and a rich gravy that made her stomach grumble louder than before. Millewa looked at Sydare embarrassed. Two people stood on the other side of the kitchen bench, beaming at them both.

"We have been waiting so long for you to come home, Millewa! Welcome, welcome" Sydare's mother, Berrima pulled Millewa tight and squeezed her until she felt she would pop. Only once had her own mother ever hugged her so tight. "Dinner is almost ready my dear, I've left some warm water by the fire for you to wash your hands and feet."

"Thanks Mum." Sydare smiled.

Dinner was delectable, a rich stew of kangaroo and carrots served on a creamy mashed potato. They drank sweet pea tea and laughed with one another, Millewa's mouth was dry from answering all the questions Berrima and Alvie threw at her about the human world.

She assisted them in cleaning up and found herself slouched in the couch, staring into the enticing fire, watching it crackle and dance. Sydare joined her and handed her a cup of lemon dew tea and a plate of petunia biscuits.

"Have you had a nice day?" Sydare asked gingerly, "I know it was very full on and we didn't get to see much."

"I am absolutely in awe, I never in my wildest dreams could've imagined any of this and you get to *live this,* every single day. I love it, I love it all" Millewa's eyes grew wider with excitement and anticipation of what was to come. "I have been waiting though, for you to tell me why I'm here."

Sydare took a deep breath and sighed. He knew the questions were inevitable and he couldn't hold her off much longer. He poured Millewa another cup of tea and watched intently as she drank deeply from her cup.

"It all started around sixteen years ago. You and I were babies and our parents were some of the most respected Elves within our land." Millewa stared open mouthed at Sydare, trying to comprehend the words he uttered. Sydare continued softly, "Sorry, I should've began with that detail. You noticed from the moment I captured you today, I saw you staring at me, gaping, continually fondling your ears as if you had a constant itch. We are Elves, small figured, pointy eared, magical beings that once solely ruled over Dewdrop Springs and the surrounding lands. Anyway, sixteen years ago a terrible tragedy occurred, King Wozil – leader of the Wizards – was murdered ferociously by orcs. Our families were visiting Clara at the time and attempted to save the city, casting spell after spell whilst the city caught alight. My Father said he had never seen a more frightening act of defiance from one creature to another. After hours of anti-flame charms and swelling water balloons, we fled, not stopping until we were back on home soil in Dewdrop Springs. Except, when we arrived, you and your family were nowhere to be seen. The flames engulfed the city and everyone in it, we assumed your family were no exception, that was, until I smelt your scent."

“My scent?” Millewa looked puzzled, trying to piece together every aspect of Sydare’s story. There were so many bits of information she had to decipher, she could feel herself becoming overwhelmed.

“You were far, but not too far that I couldn’t find you. You see, all Elves produce a unique scent that can be identified by your own clan. The moment you stepped into the Ingens Mountain region I just knew I could find you.”

“But why did you want to find me so badly? And to hold me against my will.” She became hot, suddenly realising the magnitude of her situation. Millewa had been kidnapped in broad daylight, by an Elf whom she’d just met, and trekked kilometres away from her safety net, her family. She felt faint.

“You are the key to our world, once again, being united and equal” Sydare stroked his brow, studying Millewa’s face for any kind of reaction. There was none. “Shortly after the attack of the orcs, the wizards took over the lands, demanding the Sprites and Elves work for them, slaving their fields and filling their bellies. The orcs were banished to the foothills, never to return and we are stuck providing for the true enemy of our time, Finfudune Bosmerch – The Wizard King.” Sydare looked to Millewa, before he could even get her opinion, the lemon dew tea had worked its magic and Millewa was now in a deep, dreamy sleep.

He propped a pillow beneath her sagging head and tucked the softest woollen blanket they owned, into her sides.

Chapter Five

The King's Welcome

The morning was bright and the sun was blinding as it streamed through the open window. Birds were chirping outside and the bustle of the street below was constant. Wings fluttered whilst laughter danced around the room.

Millewa opened her eyes, rubbing them gently in order to get all the sleep out. She peered around her, a couch, fireplace, kitchen and a fifty foot drop to the ground, from the top of a… tree. Millewa sat more alertly, blinking ferociously to gain her surroundings, she wasn't in her home with her numerous siblings and doting parents.

Her supposed dream of a fantasy land with sprites and elves and magic, was real.

"Registration! Registration checks here, form an orderly line folks, cmon now," a bellowing voice boomed from below the high windows.

Millewa stretched her arms and peered around the light filled room, the air was still and calm as if no one were home. She walked towards the window, placing her hands on its dark frame and casting her eyes over the edge.

"STOP!" Before she had even glanced towards the ground below, Millewa had been tackled squarely around the middle, hitting the hard flooring with a thud. Eyes wild and out of breath, Sydare sighed deeply. "I'm sorry about that, it's just, the wizards are here from Clara checking everyone's registrations".

"Registrations?" Millewa looked puzzled.

"Yes, everyone from orcs to elves must be registered with the magical council to live within Apricus. I think it's so they can keep tabs on us, you know, so we don't fall out of line with their authority." Sydare shrugged, he was used to the wizards controlling nature.

"So... If I only just found out about this place and you assumed me dead, that means..." Millewa started.

"That means you are in no way registered to live here, if Finfudune Bosmerch finds out, you are toast." Sydare bowed his head gravely, he had come to enjoy Millewa's company, her familiarity was soothing.

"When you say toast, you mean they'll send me home?" Millewa said this with a tone of amusement. Sydare had spent nearly a whole day stalking her through the forest, captured her, fed her and it could all be unravelled in a matter of minutes.

Even though she had been held against her will, Millewa had enjoyed her time here, she felt comforted in being where she was born.

"Not exactly… You know how I said Finfudune was an evil overlord?" Sydare questioned.

"Words to that effect?" Millewa smiled.

"Seriously Millewa, this isn't a time to joke. If Finfudune catches you, particularly you, he'll throw you in Mortuus or kill you."

"What is Mortuus?" Millewa's smile had faded and her fingers began to twitch, the hairs on the back of her neck were standing on edge. Her knees felt weak as she anticipated Sydare's answer.

"Mortuus is the prison in Clara. It is positioned deep below the city. I have only ever heard of its ferocity and dankness, but I also know that anyone that has gone in, rarely sees daylight ever again. It is dark, made of Rainforest Jasper stone, water continually seeps and drips onto the inhabitants, meaning you stay cold and wet and afraid. Rats nibble your toes until they are worn to nubs and your body withers to nothing due to the lack of food. I'd choose death over Mortuus." The words had barely left Sydare's lips when long fingers began tapping on the front door. Millewa and Sydare stood, frozen, eyes pinned on the door.

Tap, tap, tap, there it was again. A short yet loud knock that echoed through the large room in which they stood.

"Hello? Anyone in there? Mr and Mrs Jones, it's Barnaby Wiggledum, I didn't see you down at registration this morning so I thought I'd pay a personal visit."

Millewa and Sydare hadn't moved an inch, their breath

rapidly increasing with sweat beginning to trickle down their necks. Before they could even look to one another for guidance, Alvie came bouncing down the hall, unlatched the door and swung it open with impressive force. The situation was unavoidable now, any hope they had of hiding Millewa was utterly and unequivocally hopeless.

"Morning Wiggledum, how are you on this fine day?" Alvie had outstretched his hand and shook Barnaby Wiggledum's vigorously.

"Oh you know Mr Jones, another year passed and registration has dawned again. It took two whole days to get here this time. Those troublesome orcs were still wreaking havoc in the mountains, it seems they'll never calm down." Barnaby's face sunk, this wizard, who was tall and round with blazing red hair, looked defeated. He stroked his goatee lightly and pulled his parchment from his pockets. The parchment hovered at waist height and Wiggledum used his wand to lazily flick through the pages.

"Jones… Jones… Ah! Here you are." Wiggledum looked quite pleased, "Name and town please?"

"Alvie Jones, Dewdrop Springs" looking rather bored as he stifled a yawn, Alvie called out to his wife so she too, could register.

"Name and town please?" Wiggledum was acting as if he was reading a script.

"Berrima Jones, Dewdrop Springs" the process was then

repeated for Sydare, who quietly uttered his details, hoping Wiggledum wouldn't catch sight of Millewa. He was wrong. Just as Wiggledum had rolled his parchment and tucked it away into his belt, his eyes drifted up towards Millewa.

"Um, excuse me, but who are you?" Wiggledum knew her face, she looked scarily familiar and had stood so still he hadn't even noticed her.

"M-Millewa Cornell, sir" the words stumbled out of Millewa's mouth like a newborn foal walking for the first time. She had never felt so small or frightened in her life.

"Is that so? Well young lady, you'd better come with me. I think King Bosmerch will be very intrigued to meet you," a sly smile pulled at the corners of Wiggledum's mouth.

Millewa walked gingerly beside Wiggledum as he strode through the trees towards the town centre. She breathed slowly and gazed around her, taking in every last inch of light before she was shipped off to Mortuus.

The day was calm and bright, the perfect day if she wasn't facing imminent death and torture. How could she have been so blasé? Sydare had tried to warn her what was happening and she laughed in his face.

The centre of town was laden with elves and sprites registering, long lines filled the area, twisting upon each other in spirals of people.

Sitting high above the registration desks, was a tall, grey haired wizard who bore a grin from ear to ear, beaming down at all his magical subjects. King Finfudune Bosmerch, ruler of Apricus and head wizard of Clara. Millewa froze where she stood and stared up towards the King, he looked strong and powerful, all the things she was not.

Finfudune was scanning the crowd, showing all his teeth while he smiled. They were perfectly straight and gleaming white, with one golden fang protruding on the left side. He looked down at Millewa, a touch of surprise and intrigue crossing his face as he motioned to one of his guards to help him off his podium. Millewa gulped hard.

"I could spot you from a mile away, in a sea of elven blood" Finfudune took Millewa's hand gently in his and gave it a soft kiss. "Welcome home, Millewa Cornell."

Hushed whispers and mutters broke out amongst the surrounding crowd. The news of Millewa's return spread like wildfire through the people of Dewdrop Springs. Millewa had not yet blinked, her big, blue eyes gazing up into Finfudune's hardened face.

"I did wonder if you would ever make it back here, a terrible tragedy that rocked our world, losing your parents. Your father was an almighty man who changed the way us magic folk got along, we are forever indebted." At this, Finfudune gave a slight bow and closed his eyes. "Any who, I suppose Wiggledum has brought you to me due to the fact you are not registered with the magical council?"

Millewa nodded. "Ah yes, well that is not a worry, I have the new patron paperwork right here, we'll have it sorted in a jiffy."

"You mean; you're not throwing me in Mortuus?" Millewa finally plucked some courage in order to speak.

"Dear girl, no! We don't just throw people into our prison without good reason. You have returned home and you have every right to be here. Providing you follow our rules and keep your registration up to date, there will be no reason to lock you up." Finfudune simultaneously unfolded paperwork mid-air as he initialled and signed his sections. "Now, the only detail left is your address, where will you live?"

"Oh, well, I – uh suppose," she stammered

"With us" Berrima had followed them down to the town centre, making sure Millewa was okay. A gentle smile warmed Berrima's face and Millewa felt immense relief wash over her.

"Perfect. That is all done, I'll file it for safe keeping" Finfudune began folding the paperwork and stuffing it into his jacket when Millewa interrupted him.

"Excuse me sir, may I check over it? You know, to make sure all the information is accurate?"

"Ha ha, very much like your father! He was always double checking contracts and re-reading information. You must forgive me, I have known you since you were a baby, naturally, I know all your details" Finfudune gave her a sweet smile. It was hard for Millewa to believe that this man had caused unrest amongst the lands.

Once Millewa's registration was dated and signed, she shook

hands with Finfudune and thanked him for his generosity. He reminded her to follow the laws put in place by Wizarding Orders and Township (W.O.T) and implored her to visit the local library where copies of their law book were kept.

She turned on her heel and skipped her way back to Sydare's house.

Millewa was only just out of sight when Finfudune's smile turned to a grave frown, his teeth no longer gleaming and his eyes no longer bright. The pale green irises had now turned black and deep lines creased his face.

"Keep an eye on her, her reappearance needs to be short lived. I want her gone and fast. Do it swiftly and make it look like another creature has slayed her." Finfudune turned to his head guard, Neptune, his thick set body and dull eyes bearing down on Finfudune's smaller frame.

"Sir, you saw the crowd reaction today, Fenwick Cornell was their leader and friend; they love her, they respect her. How do you expect me to make this look like an accident?" Neptune shrugged.

"I don't care who they love and what they do" Finfudune snarled. He shot his wand straight up in the air, a lightning bolt erupting from the tip. The sky darkened with clouds and rain began to fall. Elves and sprites around them fled indoors, leaving the town centre barren.

"Kill them all if you have to."

Chapter Six

The Amarok

Millewa had now been in Dewdrop Springs for two days. She had seen nothing but the town square and its shops, and the four spacious rooms that made up Sydare's luxurious home. Berrima and Alvie had set the spare room for Millewa whilst she was being registered and had magically made the room of her dreams. Dark green walls with shimmering gold leaves and vines. The chocolatey wooden floor was softened by a cream coloured wool rug. Her bed had four posts and long, heavy drapes that spilt over the sides, encasing it like a darkened cave. It was perfect and everything she had ever hoped for.

Meandering down the hall, Millewa ran her fingers along the thin, oak tables that lined the walls, she must've walked this way a dozen times. Countless glass containers like huge pickle jars littered the tables filled with thick green goo. Millewa jumped, letting out a small squeal as she clasped her hands over her mouth.

The jars were not only filled with green goo, but each jar was home to a head, Elven heads that blinked lazily at Millewa as she gaped. She could only assume this was Sydare's dead relatives, wiping away a layer of dust from the rusted name label that read: *Ella Jones*.

Millewa stared at the faces, tracing the jar outline when suddenly, she noticed a blink. Taken aback, Millewa repeated her motion and traced the outline. Another blink.

"How curious" she whispered at the face.

"Actually, it isn't curious at all. Have you never seen a family memorial before my dear?" Alvie's mother's head was staring at Millewa with her eyebrows raised, looking disapprovingly down her nose.

"I haven't actually, are you… are you dead?"

"What a stupid question, clearly from a very stupid girl. Of course I'm dead you nitwit, how else do you think my severed head would be talking? The nerve of you!" Millewa slowly backed away towards the kitchen, holding eye contact with Ella Jones until she could no longer see her ferocious eyes.

Sydare was already at the breakfast table, reading a thick book whilst munching on cereal. The box beside him read 'Crunchy Wand-os'.

"Your grandma is a scary lady" Millewa exclaimed as she grabbed herself a bowl from the cupboard.

"She's not very friendly is she?" milk spat everywhere as Sydare spoke and Millewa had to refrain from crinkling her face in disgust. "She's even mean to me every time I walk past. '*Why haven't you grown? What's that smell? Tuck that hair behind your ears,'* it's honestly never ending."

"What are 'Crunchy Wand-os'?" Millewa picked up the box and began examining the packaging. She'd never seen cereal like this before.

"Oh I keep forgetting you live amongst humans. It's just like regular human cereal, except instead of fruity rings, they're fruity wizard wands. Pretty cool, huh?"

Millewa shrugged and poured herself a large helping. As the cereal fell from the box, small sparks flew from the end of the fruity wands, creating tiny fireworks in her bowl.

"Woah." Millewa gaped. Sydare smiled. "What's the plan for today then?"

"Well, I have a whole day of touring and surprises planned. Are you in?"

"You bet." Millewa grinned.

"Not so fast, Sydare. Aren't you forgetting something?" Alvie had appeared out of nowhere, leaning against the kitchen counter and rapping his fingers against the bench.

"Oh," Sydare slumped. "I did forget. Do I have to today, Dad? Millewa has been here two days and has barely seen a thing. I promise to double time next week!" Millewa looked from Sydare to Alvie, neither of them said a word and argued silently across the room.

The air was tense and uncomfortable.

"I'm afraid not" Alvie finally said after minutes of pure, silent torture. Sydare rolled his eyes and exited the room, slamming his bedroom door with a loud thud.

"Sorry Millewa, Sydare has training today and it cannot be missed. He will only be an hour or two, feel free to roam the house or the town square" Alvie offered a sweet smile and gestured her to leave the kitchen.

There was no way she was staying in the house with Ella Jones and with that she took the pulley down to the ground floor and began exploring the expansive vegetable patch.

Rows and rows of fruits and vegetables blanketed the front garden, an array of colour carpeting the soil beneath. The air smelt crisp and fresh, flowers sprouting and forming fruit in quick succession. There were self-harvesting peach trees that collected the fruit in wicker baskets at the base of the trunk, singing cucumber vines that you could give a tune to repeat and lavender sprouted in between the berries, alerting a hoard of bees to it.

Meandering through the gooseberry bushes, Millewa ran her hands along the top of the leaves, letting the softness tickle her fingertips, a thorn pricking the end of her finger. She looked at it, a small trickle of blood pooling at the point. She studied her finger intently, not hearing the pulley system of the house starting to drag, the chain aching as it descended down the tree.

Millewa could hear hushed voices, talking rapidly. Without another thought, she tucked her body and rolled behind the prized giant cabbages, peering through their outer leaves to see Sydare and Alvie emerge from the tree base.

Sydare's face was concentrated and hard, listening intently to every word Alvie said. Millewa couldn't hear what they were saying, but she knew it wasn't good. Impulsively, she began to follow them, staying out of sight and ensuring her footsteps were as quiet as a mouse.

A wall of thick trunked trees separated the garden bed and the path in which they followed, Millewa ducked behind bushes and scrambled branches to stay hidden.

"Why is this training so necessary, Dad?" Sydare asked, looking around wildly for signs of life.

"Well, The King's presence in Dewdrop Springs yesterday sparked quite the controversy amongst our people. They believe extra training is needed in order to stay vigilant. It's not every day Finfudune shows his face, it was quite alarming, we need to be prepared." Alvie kept his head forward, looking unblinkingly at the path ahead.

"I see..." Sydare considered this and shrugged, shuffling his feet as they pressed on. Moments later, they entered a huge clearing, far bigger than the town square and larger than the football oval at Millewa's school.

The field was mostly open and flat, grass covering the majority of the area. There were small sections of dirt where the grass had died and where at least thirty men stood in line, weapons in hands.

Millewa gazed around, taking in more as each minute passed. Huge wooden structures stood tall above the elves. Some were shaped in a 'V' and looked as though they were required to climb it, another was an extensive mud pit that bubbled and shrieked, but what scared Millewa the most, was two large steel doors leading into the side of the hill. A deep, angry growl erupting from its opening, the doors shaking in fear from what was inside.

It wasn't just a field or large oval, it was a training battle ground and Alvie was leading the charge in today's training session. Millewa gaped as he approached the elves, waiting patiently for him to arrive, all standing to attention, faces stern.

"Shall we begin" Alvie stood tall and fierce as his comrades dispersed, sprinting to the various drill stations. "GO!" A loud boom echoed from all directions and the well-oiled machine of warriors began their warm up. They seemed to start by climbing the 'V' wall, then a huge lap around the perimeter, a crawl through the mud pit and finally finishing by shooting a flaming arrow through a hanging hoop.

Millewa's eyes couldn't keep up with the mass of elves moving in synchronisation and with utter grace, one after the other they completed the drills.

Sydare was flawless, like an eagle soaring high above the air, he moved with an aura of elegance and dexterity that distinguished him from the rest, no one could match him, nor did they try.

Millewa readjusted her positioning on the edge of the clearing and watched in awe. Only once Alvie called them all back did they retreat from their posts, standing in neat, even formation on the dirt patch.

"Today is slightly different," Alvie addressed his soldiers, "normally we would run drills, you would practise your skills and we would refine our techniques. But, not today. In this session, you will watch, you will take mental notes and you will learn, learn as if your life depends on it, because it does. Sydare?" Sydare stepped forward from the pack, shoulders broad and strong, he faced his father, emotionless.

"I am ready, sir." Sydare gave a small nod to Alvie.

"Release it." Alvie gave a wave of his hand, a strong, calculated movement that had every elf staring, waiting.

A slow, screeching creak reverberated through Millewa's body, a shiver crawling up her spine as the giant steel doors carved into the hill, began to open. The air was tense and silent. No one dared say a word or move.

Footsteps that landed with a great thud grew louder, making its way towards them. Sydare drew his sword, its silver edging gleaming in the light, daring to blind anyone who looked at it. Another loud thud. Millewa could see his eyes closing, his breaths were long and slow.

Thud.

She couldn't bear to watch, Sydare was only sixteen and whatever was coming sounded far too dangerous for him to handle alone. Alvie believed he could do it, so, so should she. A final booming thud sent shockwaves through the ground, like an earthquake had rippled through the clearing. A menacing growl and a vision of pointy, yellowed teeth that bared themselves to the open court.

The other elves cowered in shock and disbelief, one elf slowly backing away, trying to reach tree cover before the beast emerged. Sydare braced his legs, a slight sway as he patiently waited for the attack.

It was quicker than lightning with more force than a tsunami. Millewa would've missed what it looked like had she blinked any longer than a millisecond.

A gigantic, wolf like creature, with mangy grey fur and thick foaming gums. Its eyes were blacker than the night sky, whilst its teeth gleamed a putrid yellow that gnashed at Sydare as he attempted his defence. He seemed powerless against such a beast, but his face remained neutral and focussed as they circled one another, their eyes and gaze not wavering.

Millewa noticed on the back of the wolfs neck, a bright emerald stone protruded, but it didn't look like it was hanging there, but rather it was *attached* to the dog in some way, controlling its every move.

"My warriors, *this* is the latest weapon in Finfudune's arsenal. The Amarok. Watch now as Sydare demonstrates how to disarm, maim and kill such an animal." Alvie puffed his chest out, he clearly felt proud that Sydare was leading the demonstration today, proving to the strongest elves, that Sydare was capable of such an enormous feat. Millewa felt sick.

Sydare stalked the Amarok, twirling his sword, mesmerizing

the beast into submission. But the Amarok would not bow down so easily.

A loud pop, and the Amarok disappeared from its spot, only to reappear moments later, behind Sydare. Its large teeth spitting and drooling as it prowled closer to the back of Sydare. The Amarok lifted himself onto his hind legs, gearing up and preparing to pounce.

Sydare turned just in time.

He ducked and rolled from beneath the beast, latching onto his tail with all his might. Sydare hung from the Amarok, flailing as it thrashed around, trying to shake him off. The Amarok's back legs were kicking frantically, its head at a distorted angle trying to bite Sydare.

Sydare was relentless, dodging and weaving, cutting chunks of fur with him as he went. The Amarok squealed as Sydare's blade connected with flesh, a small stream of blood dribbled down its leg, staining its grey fur. It ferociously slammed its paws to the ground, the shockwave sending Sydare flying across the field and landing with an almighty crash.

The Amarok turned.

His eyes wild with fury and hatred. His upper lip curled into an enraged snarl. He wasted no time and sprinted at Sydare. His eyes locked on Sydare, unrelenting, he chased him down.

Millewa noticed a slight quiver in Sydare and it was hard to believe this sixteen-year-old elf was fighting against an ancient beast.

The Amarok let out a supreme howl as he jumped high in the air, his body covering Sydare completely as he landed.

That's when the screaming began.

Blood curdling.

High pitched.

Something was dying. Millewa had to look away, the sound too much for her to handle, the smell of blood overwhelming her nose. All she could hear was flesh being ripped and torn and bones crunching under immense weight. Only when the screaming stopped did she look back.

Sydare stood, proudly, atop the Amarok holding the emerald jewel from its neck, his sword protruding from the centre, its weak spot.

Cheers and claps erupted from the warrior elves, gazing at Sydare with adoration. He had done it. He had done it all by himself. Sydare beamed at his peers and slid down the side of the beast, walking his way to the crowd. Only then did Millewa see the damage that had been done to the Amarok and the mutilation that had taken place. The Amarok had been skinned alive. Its face distorted with chunks of flesh missing and bones sticking out at odd angles. Its feet had been severed to prevent it from running and its teeth had been plucked clean, one by one.

Millewa stared and felt remorse for the poor animal, whispering 'I'm sorry' as she turned to walk back to the town centre.

The whole ordeal she had encountered this morning, she

decided to keep to herself, not sharing with Sydare that she had followed them. She shuffled away and replayed the fight in her head over and over again.

The Amarok was strong, but Sydare was a trained killer.

Chapter Seven

The Treaty of Murder

Millewa sprinted back to the house, quickly pulled herself up the pulley and sat on the couch, grabbing a book on her way in, pretending she hadn't moved all morning. Sydare limped into the house, bypassing Millewa and heading straight for the bathroom.

Once Sydare returned after bathing, and Grandma Ella stopped shouting at them, Sydare and Millewa packed a backpack each. Sydare carried blankets, fireball starters and two pillow poppers, which were the size of a match box until you popped them and they became regular sized.

Millewa had boxes of freshly cut fruits, bottles of lemonade fizzers and two containers of walnut ravioli. She was salivating already at the thought.

It was surprisingly calm and quiet for mid-morning. There were very few elves around in the main square. Sydare's training finished as soon as he defeated the Amarok and they could get on with their day.

The fountain bubbled and splashed, the pavement around it

becoming damp. There was no sign that it had even rained the night before.

Millewa clasped the straps on her backpack and took a deep breath in, fresh bakery bread and damp grass filled her nostrils, the sun warming her cheeks. They wandered through the town square at a snail pace, taking in the beautiful morning, as more and more elves began emerging from the trees and bushes.

Suddenly, Sydare came to a halt, stopping dead in his tracks. Millewa, who wasn't paying attention bumped into his back and nearly fell.

"Stop one, we're here!" exclaimed Sydare.

Millewa looked up, a grand oak building that looked as if it had been carved straight out of an enormous tree stood before her. Copper stained windows dotted the outside, whilst a warm glow emanated from within. A giant gold sign hung above the door, read: *The Dewdrop Memorial Library.* A small plaque marked the door: *In Loving Memory of Fenwick & Alma.*

Millewa touched it slightly, a tingle rippling through her fingertips.

"How could you have possibly known that the library was my utmost favourite place in the human world?" Millewa asked in awe.

"Intuition I guess, would you like to head inside?" Sydare pushed open the heavy, double doors that lead inside.

If Millewa thought the outside was magnificent, it was nothing compared to what was inside. High walls as far as the eye could see, covered in shelves and books. The circular inside had every genre imaginable.

The librarian was hard at work, whisking between elves at the desk, fulfilling their borrowing needs. He was a stern looking elf, with dark eyes and long bleached dreadlocks that hung freely at his sides. Millewa watched as he danced around the main library, waving his hands swiftly as books collapsed from the shelves into neat piles. The librarian's eyes darted about the room until they landed squarely on Millewa, the dark brown irises piercing through her.

"Millewa Cornell, I never thought I'd see the day where you set foot in this library," the librarian bowed, so low his dreadlocks almost grazed the ground. "It is an honour to meet you".

"It is nice to meet you too… sir. How is it you know who I am though?" Millewa was puzzled. She knew her father was the Elven leader but was starting to wonder what kind of influence he had over the people.

"You, are quite well known amongst the Elves. Your father was an incredible man and did many great things for us. We all hoped you had survived so you too could continue his reign. I am Hillard, memorial librarian, scholar and a loyal subject of the Cornell family." Hillard smiled down at Millewa, his once ferocious eyes now kind and warm.

"Anything you ever need, please don't hesitate to check in with me. Here, take this, it will inform you on how truly special your parents were." A heavy, leather-bound book landed with a thud at Millewa's feet.

She smiled at Hillard, grasped the book and scurried out the door without glancing back.

"That elf *never* gives books away, especially without a library pass, give us a look at it," Sydare stared at the book intently and gave a small frown as he turned it over in his hands. "I'd better carry this, it'll be way too heavy and we have a long way to go."

"I'm more than capable of carrying it" Millewa scowled, she didn't like being told she can't do something.

"Oh, Millewa, no I didn't mean it like that, I just mean, you're carrying everything pretty much and it wouldn't be fair to throw this big old book in there too" Sydare stuttered. Millewa gave him an unsure look and shrugged, there was no point arguing over it and wasting their day.

Sydare continued his tour, showing Millewa all the old buildings in Dewdrop Springs that once made up the old town square. The jail, book store and cobbler were a few of the more notable stops.

It was nearing lunch time and Millewa could feel her stomach rumbling, they had been walking and talking all morning and had forgotten to eat any of the snacks they'd packed.

Finally, after trekking through shrubs and bushes for what seemed like an hour, Millewa and Sydare stumbled upon a clear, wide lagoon that was powdered blue and sparkling beneath the sunlight. Millewa took a deep inhale and closed her eyes, letting the sun warm her cheeks. Trees canopied the water's edge providing much needed shade.

As Millewa took in her surroundings, Sydare began setting up in a nearby cave. He popped the pillow poppers and cracked the fireball starters, a warm flame erupting from the packages. With care, the blankets were laid out and the fruit presented deliciously on a platter. Millewa's mouth was salivating as she dropped her pack and rushed over to devour the treats.

It was the perfect way to finish what had been a near perfect day, they swam and ate, then swam again, then ate again until the sun began setting over the mountains and they were too exhausted to move from their cave camp.

"This has been the best day ever" Millewa was grinning ear to ear.

As night settled in, the once blue lagoon began to illuminate a deep bottle green that had flecks of all different colours rippling through the surface. Purples, greens and yellows danced across the water, brightening and darkening within seconds. Millewa was in awe of the beauty, gazing at their own personal light show.

She turned to see if Sydare was as impressed as her, but when she faced him, he had fallen asleep. Millewa popped a blanket over him as he did her first night and smiled at her first ever real friend.

Millewa tossed and turned all night on the banks of the lagoon, willing herself to sleep without any success. Millewa sat bolt upright, sick of attempting to sleep, she reached for Sydare's backpack and from it slipped the huge book she had been gifted from Hillard the librarian. She flipped the pages lazily, tracing the pictures with her fingers until she came across a new chapter a quarter of the way through, titled: *The Modern History – Wozil's defeat, Finfudune's reign and the enslavement and capture of Elves and Sprites.* Millewa's eyes widened, the history of her family and how they died was at the tip of her fingertips.

Sydare stirred and grumbled as he rolled to face the other way, Millewa had noticed Sydare's reluctance for her to read the book and now was her chance to have ample, uninterrupted time.

Slowly and stealthily, Millewa slipped out from under her blanket, clasping the book tightly under her arm, her eyes unwavering from Sydare and silently pleading with him to stay asleep. She backed away slowly, grabbing a fireball starter and swiftly turning to run into the thick brush.

Finding a large tree to perch under, she cracked the fireball starter and her small, secluded area erupted with light. The forest was eerily silent, only the wind whistling through the treetops could be heard. Millewa propped the book up and began to read, page by page, chapter by chapter, until she had read it cover to cover twice, trying to make sense of it all.

She couldn't comprehend it.

"Quite a past we have" Sydare's voice cut through the night like a knife. Millewa almost jumped out of her skin as she turned to see Sydare baring over her with wide eyes.

"All those things, did they really happen?" Millewa's eye began to fill with tears, she knew her parents died trying to save

Clara, what she didn't realise was the aftermath and consequence of their deaths.

"I tried to protect you from this. I tried to keep that book away from you, from revealing the truth, saving you from the fact that your parents death caused the biggest enslavement our kind has seen. You had to go snooping, you had to ruin the perfect day we had. Our freedom was stolen and the treaty abolished because Fenwick had to go and get himself killed." Sydare's eyes were filled with fire, his breath hot as he spat the words at Millewa.

She was furious.

Sydare had purposely hidden this from her and her blood boiled.

"How dare you. How dare you blame my dead family. From what I have read, the death of King Wozil was a terrible tragedy, but it also doesn't sound like it was completely accidental and I certainly don't think the orcs are to blame.

"Did you know that Finfudune Bosmerch was the King's advisor prior to his death? You would think this would mean that once King Wozil had died, Finfudune would automatically take his place, wouldn't you? Well, according to the treaty written by magical leaders, this rule was abandoned due to too many assassinations of past kings. So why did Finfudune come to power, if this was written in the Treaty of Peace? Oh that's right, all the magical leaders who signed were murdered in quick succession after the fact." Millewa felt her face getting hot, her face reddening with every quickened breath.

She was angry. Furious.

There was a reason Hillard had given her that book, a message, a warning of what was coming her way. "So of course Finfudune came to power, when no one could stand up and tell him he was wrong. The orcs were banished without a second thought and they suddenly became the most hated creatures in the land, convenient for Finfudune.

"The heat was off him long enough for him to implement a slave trade amongst elves and sprites, we were doomed no matter what, no matter if my father had been killed or not. Finfudune Bosmerch wanted power and by golly did he get it. I think it is no accident, in fact, I think he planned it all, to the very last detail he knew what he was doing." Sydare gaped at Millewa. Millewa could see he wanted to speak but words wouldn't come out of his mouth.

Millewa knew there was truth to what she said. Finfudune Bosmerch was a murderous tyrant. It was written all over Sydare's face.

Chapter Eight

All Those in Favour

The air was tense when Millewa and Sydare awoke the next morning. The mist was only just lifting from the chilled waters, whilst the sun broke through the trees and tickled their faces as they packed up their camp. They had gone to sleep without a word last night and neither one of them had the courage to speak first that morning.

Their first fight.

Their first disagreement.

Millewa really hoped they could overcome this hiccup, she hoped the damage hadn't run too deep.

By the time they had slowly packed away their things and had slung their backpacks over their shoulders, the sun beat down on them unrelenting and harsh. Millewa had been stewing all morning on how to approach her most recent concerns with Sydare, but she wasn't quite sure how to do it. She bit her tongue and sheepishly faced him, her hands twisting in knots trying to say the words.

Finally, with a deep breath, she muttered:

"I – I want to see my family again" her voice wasn't as brave or as bold as she had wished.

"Millewa, we went through this yesterday. Your family is dead; don't you remember when you attacked me so abruptly?" Sydare's words cut through Millewa and she winced as he shot daggers at her.

He was obviously still upset with what had occurred the night previous.

"No, no, no. Not my biological family. My human family. The family that has raised me since I was no bigger than a packet of flour. They will surely be missing me and I need to know that they're okay. Do you think I can go back?" Millewa's bottom lip quivered at the thought.

She had been so caught up in what she'd been doing, seeing the land, exploring old buildings and trying exotic foods, she had completely forgotten to even think about the family she had left behind.

Her kind, loving foster parents and her all too rowdy siblings, even though they were mean to her, she still missed them dearly.

"Oh… yes that family. I won't be able to arrange for you to meet them, but I can certainly open a portal that will allow you to view them live" Sydare had sweat dripping down his face, his smile shaky. He didn't want Millewa to leave, he'd only just found her and was enjoying her company, despite their disagreement.

"You mean, like a livestream of my family? Where I can view but not interact?" Sydare nodded his head in agreeance, it wasn't what she was thinking but it would do.

The walk back to Dewdrop Springs town seemed a lot shorter this time around. Both Sydare and Millewa had a spring in their step and mostly skipped the whole way back. After an initial awkward fifteen minutes, the two were back talking, dancing and singing like there was no issue at all.

Millewa was glad to see Sydare smiling again, but more so she was excited to have her best friend back. Imagine that, *best friend*, Millewa had never had one friend in her life and now she had one that she relied on for everything.

Once back home in the comfort of the tree, Millewa perched herself on the couch and slumped immediately, succumbing to the soft, squishy pillows.

She watched as Sydare fiddled about with potion bottles and sparkly dust that was filed neatly in a wooden box. His face hardened as he focused on each individual vial and held them to the light as if he were trying to decipher the contents.

"I'm not terribly confident in portals I'm afraid, but I'm sure I'll be able to connect to them" he continued fiddling away with the vials and shaking them to disperse the liquids and dusts.

"That's okay, anything to see my family again" Millewa gave him a small smile, she could see he was trying and that was all she could ask.

"What's this then?" Alvie's voice entered the room before he did. His slim figure sauntered into the room, green linen pants flowing and swishing as his eyes focused on Millewa. "What is this I hear of portal conjuring, Sydare?" Alvie's green eyes shifted to Sydare, an eyebrow raised disapprovingly.

"Uh – hi Dad. Millewa asked if she could see her family, I explained to her that she cannot be sent back or interact but that we can conjure a portal so she can view them and see how they're doing. I hope this is okay." Sydare's eyes did not meet his fathers. His feet shuffled the ground as he shifted weight from side to side. Alvie's face considered this for a moment, his lips twitching before finally he said:

"Fine. But you'd best move over Sydare, that's powerful magic you're playing with."

Alvie tinkered with the jars of sparkle and bottles, just as Sydare had been doing. Within five minutes he had mixed various colours, liquids and dusts in a large pot, that was now steaming with gold flecks popping and splattering as the mixture bubbled. Alvie gave a small, proud smile as he began his incantation.

"Human world to which we speak, hear us now. John and Stella are who we seek, use this portal as it is. Let us see them, let us hear them for the greater power is." Alvie kept his eyes closed, arms outstretched and hands moving swiftly as the room began to change.

A swirl of black and golden light filled the room, long strokes of smoke danced through the air. A warm breeze touched Millewa's nose as the room around them disappeared.

Instead, an image of her home, her original home, came to life. The dusty floorboards, the chaos and, what she had been waiting for, her parents John and Stella. They were standing in the kitchen, working around one another in perfect synchrony whilst cooking. Stella and John loved to cook together and they were currently cooking the family's favourite meal: breakfast. Millewa's eyes stung as she could feel them swelling with tears, she missed them dearly and hadn't realised until she saw them, standing right in front of her, so close yet so incredibly far away.

Quite suddenly, noise began erupting from the frame they could see. Loud sizzling sausages and the clank of tongs against the pans. John and Stella were talking. They were talking about Millewa.

"I never knew losing Millewa could change our lives so drastically," Stella reported to John who was now scrambling the eggs. Millewa felt her heart sink. This would be really hard on them, their favourite foster child, ripped away from them in a never ending forest.

"I completely agree," John replied "I'm so thankful to be rid of that little brat. Our lives *have* changed, for the better." The words cut through Millewa like a knife.

She continued to watch as more of her family members entered the room, celebrating the disappearance of Millewa and how happy they were for her to be gone. She couldn't believe her eyes and she couldn't believe her ears. Had she been so blind to believe that they had actually loved her? Like really, actually loved her? How could they, she *was* a freak. She *was* all the nasty things those bullies called her.

Millewa began to cry. Sobbing uncontrollably into her hands, tears streaming down her cheeks in a constant flow.

"Well, that settles it then doesn't it?" Millewa looked up from her hands and into Sydare's kind and caring face. "If I'm not wanted there, I don't ever want to go back."

"This is your home, where you were born and we are so excited to have you back," Sydare smiled at Millewa, a large, genuine smile that made her tears stop. She smiled back and hugged him. A warm, tight hug, Millewa's life could now finally begin without a worry if she would ever be good enough.

"Sydare, would you mind if I had a word with your father for a minute? There's just some questions I have." Sydare nodded and promptly walked down the hallway, his grandmother's head shouting at him as he passed.

Alvie sat on the couch, waiting for Millewa to speak about what had been bothering her.

She was hard pressed to find the words. She had been given so much information about her parents, particularly her father, yet she felt like there was something missing. Something wasn't quite right and she needed to talk to the one person her family trusted more than anyone else.

"Alvie, what really happened to my mother and father? I've read through the books I've been given and listened to varying stories. Clara was showered in fire and both my parents didn't make it home. What I can't seem to understand is, why them? Why were they killed? Did anyone ever find their bodies?" Millewa blubbered the words and looked at Alvie with bright eyes filled with tears. Now that she had no human family to go back to, she felt immensely sad for the one she had lost in the magical world.

"It is true that Clara burst into a ring of fire the night King Wozil was murdered and it is rumoured Finfudune orchestrated the whole event in order to ascend the throne. Your father was one of the four kingdom leaders of Apricus; alongside the orcs, wizards and sprites, your father was one of the most powerful beings in the lands. He worked with a council of people in Dewdrop Springs that were in charge of decision making. Your father would then present this to the kingdom leaders at regular meetings, as they would with their land requests. It was harmonious. It was glorious. Wozil, Cornell, Quentin and Serrell were the names we knew and trusted to handle all the lands dealings, they were strong, compassionate and excellent leaders. We lived in peace during their reign." Alvie took a sip of water and continued.

"Obviously that all changed very quickly. When meetings were held, you could see Finfudune becoming increasingly restless, whispering in Wozil's ear trying to push his agenda, Wozil simply waved his hand and refused to put forward his ideas. This seemed to anger Finfudune. I watched him closely each time we met, trying to gauge what he wanted. It was only once I sat down with Fenwick that he informed me of Finfudune's wishes. He believed wizards were a superior being and should have far more control over the kingdoms than the rest of us. He was pushing Wozil to abolish the Treaty of Peace and put forward a motion of dictatorship, of which Wozil did not comply."

"Is that when… he… killed them?" Millewa interrupted.

"It has not been proven that Finfudune murdered our leaders, nor has it been disproven. This back and forth went on for months, when finally, at the meeting in February before the Autumn markets, your father stood in front of council and announced Finfudune's grand plans. Revealing everything he was hoping and planning, exposing him as a monster to the rest of the kingdom. As you can imagine, this didn't go down well with the others at all. Quentin, the Sprite leader scoffed and turned his back, refusing to face Finfudune for the atrocity he was being accused of. Serrell, the orc leader however, took a much more aggressive approach, blaming Wozil for allowing Finfudune to continue in council, spitting and slashing his teeth in protest.

"I remember it as clear as day how angry that orc was. Lucky your father was able to mediate and calm everyone down, Finfudune seething at being exposed. That was the last time they were all in the one place. The Autumn markets rolled around and Finfudune's wish came true and life as we knew it changed from peace to enslavement and working for the wizards, rather than *with* them." Alvie gave a deep sigh and bowed his head, almost as if he was praying.

“So, really it was between the orcs and Finfudune that could’ve killed Wozil and destroyed Clara. They both showed their intentions and had motive to do so.” Millewa had a puzzled look on her face, trying to piece it all together.

Alvie had answered so many questions, but with influx of information, more questions continued to arise.

“That is how it seems, yes.” Alvie still kept his head low.

“All of Clara burned?” Millewa posed.

“Yes, every edge of the city” Alvie replied.

“The bodies of my parents?” Millewa was afraid of the answer.

“We found remains of your father in the main street, he was near dust when I found him” Alvie looked as if he could throw up, the memory flashing in his eyes.

“And my mother?” Millewa looked pleadingly into Alvie’s eyes, looking for some sort of emotion or admission. Alvie shifted his gaze from the floor to Millewa, studying her face, just as Sydare had done the first time they met. His reply sad yet cold.

“We searched. For days. There was no sign she was even there.”

Chapter Nine

The Sapphire Pool

Millewa slept restlessly that night. She tossed and turned playing the scenario over in her mind continuously. Her father was dead and it was as if her mother never existed, vanished into thin air. Millewa's mind raced with the possibilities and what she was going to do next. Finfudune is believed to be evil, but so are the orcs and her mother might be alive, but she might not.

She contemplated the options: did she talk to Finfudune and try to regain elf freedom? Or did she search for her potentially alive mother? She threw her face against her pillow and screamed. It was all too overwhelming. Not realising how loud she yelled, Sydare was now standing in her doorway, leaning casually against the frame.

"Couldn't sleep, huh?" Sydare asked calmly as he went and sat in the swinging chair that dangled just outside her window.

"Not a wink." Millewa replied "I can't stop thinking about the conversation I had with your dad. He gave me a lot to think about and now I'm sitting here, mind foggy, trying to figure out what to do."

"Lucky for you, young Millewa, I was eavesdropping the whole time you spoke to dad" Sydare grinned uncontrollably, his pointed ears twitching with excitement. "Now, tell me the issue and how we can potentially resolve it."

Millewa explained to Sydare where her mind was at. The confusion of her mum, the battle between the orcs and Finfudune and who was really at fault and whether or not she chases freedom or family.

Millewa watched Sydare as she spoke, his sombre posture, his intent stare as he lingered on her every word. Only after she had completely finished speaking did Sydare offer his advice.

"You certainly haven't made this easy on me, have you?" Sydare twiddled his thumbs and looked longingly at Millewa, "I think I may have an idea though, or at least some advice on what I think the best option is."

"Anything will be helpful at this point in time" Millewa's head lowered, a tight knot forming in her chest. This decision was constricting her, her judgement clouded by what is right and what is preferred.

"Well," Sydare started. "You said it yourself, your mother is missing but isn't confirmed to be alive or dead, correct?"

"Correct" Millewa replied.

"But Finfudune, the orcs, they *are* alive and they *are* accessible." Sydare looked grimly at Millewa. "I know the temptation is to go looking for your mum, but you could be looking for years. Think about it, Clara is only a two-day trek and you could confront Finfudune and this could all be over, then you could search for your mum. But to search for your mum before demanding salvation, well, selfishly, the elves are ready to take their lives back and so far you're the only one strong enough to do so."

Millewa considered him for a moment, tossing all the ideas around in her head and thinking deeply about what Sydare said. He was right, it would be selfish for her to pursue her mother, that still didn't make it any easier.

And her? Strong enough?

She had felt nothing but inadequate since she had arrived in Apricus and Dewdrop Springs, how could she really be the one to save the elves?

"You're right." Millewa stared at Sydare intensely, "it wouldn't be right and hey, if Finfudune agrees, I could be looking for mum as soon as Saturday. So, how do we do this?"

"Well, we have to plan, like really plan" Sydare said sombrely "I've only shown you about Dewdrop Springs, nothing further beyond our safety barrier. You have no idea what terror lies beyond the barrier and we need to ensure we're ready."

"Where do we start?" Millewa puffed out her chest bravely and stood tall, she needed to be ready for anything and if that meant pretending she wasn't scared out of her wits, that's what she would do.

"We need to take today, grab some food and go far where

nosey pointed ears cannot hear us. Then we can put together our plan of attack." Sydare said in a hushed voice.

By the time Millewa and Sydare had packed a bag and gathered some food from the cupboards, as they had done so many times before, the town of Dewdrop Springs was alive with hustle and bustle of elves and sprites.

The streets were pulsating with footsteps and the chatter of elves was electric like a swarm of bees. Shops had already put out their street displays, intending to persuade shoppers to buy their wares. The Menders already had a line of fifteen or more, ready to be cured of whatever illness they carried. The sky was clear and not a cloud dared to intrude on the perfect blue.

Millewa pointed her face to the sky and felt the warmth wash over her. It was still only morning and soon the sun would beat down on them like stinging lava, too hot to stand out and enjoy.

Millewa felt Sydare tug her arm, she opened her eyes and looked at him, his head jerked to the side silently indicating for her to get moving.

She rolled her eyes and adjusted her backpack, surely five minutes in the sunshine wouldn't have hurt them, but she moved swiftly in step with him as they made way for the thicket of cascading trees that led to an unknown area, Millewa hadn't dared to go and see.

It felt as though they had been walking for hours, exhaustion had set in early once the sun began beaming down on their skin. Its hot fury prickling at every uncovered inch as they reddened under the cloudless sky. Millewa could feel the sweat dripping from her brow, drying before it even had a chance to trickle down her burning face. She had to tie her hair in two small plaits to give her neck relief from the sticky strands that strangled her as they walked. She had never experienced heat like this, she had never felt so depleted and dehydrated as she did right now and she urged her feet to keep pushing, hoping their rest point was only a few more minutes away.

Her tongue clicked, trying to suck any moisture that may have been left and becoming bitterly disappointed when only dryness consumed her mouth.

"Sydare, please, let us stop. I feel every part of me is without water and I need a break" Millewa pleaded with Sydare as he kept a strong pace out in front, walking so quickly, Millewa was almost jogging to keep up with him. Who knew little legs such as his could produce such an impressive stride.

As if her words floated off in the air, Sydare ignored her and kept his head forward, a scowl upon his face and his hands wrapped around his backpack strap. Millewa had not seen Sydare behave like this before and thought it best to stay behind him and keep quiet.

What felt like an eternity to Millewa and her decaying senses, it was only a matter of moments before they arrived at their destination. Millewa gaped at the landscape as Sydare removed his backpack and announced they'd made it. It never ceased to amaze her how beautiful the lands of Apricus were and this was no exception.

Large rocks and boulders shouldered the earth, creating a valley to which a small stream trickled its way between the crevasses. Smooth, slippery rocks butted against one another, forming dips and climbs. Dark moss coated lower boulders, providing nutrients for the animals that frequented this place.

Millewa dropped her pack and walked towards to a mass of rock and stone, pressing her face against its cool surface, she sighed with relief as her amber cheeks began to chill, a biting sensation as the two elements met. As she rolled her face off the closest rock, Sydare walked towards her with an oak leaf, full of blue shimmering water that he had scooped from a nearby pool. Millewa drank the liquid gratefully and felt her mind clear as the cool water travelled through her body, hydrating every limb.

"Over here, Millewa. I want to show you something" Sydare gestured to Millewa, his eyes sparkling under the sunlight seeping through the canopy of trees. Millewa could see just beyond him there was a small hole in the rocks, filled with dark blue water that rippled with the light winds caress.

"What is this?" Millewa said as she stared at the pool. The hole would barely fit either one of them, their shoulders would surely scrape the sides. The water looked so inviting, the sun beared down on their backs and Millewa felt sweat trickling down her face once more.

"Do you trust me?" Sydare grinned cheekily at Millewa, outstretching his hand to her.

"Yes, I do" and with all her heart, Millewa meant that.

From the moment they had met, Sydare had been honest with her, taken her in when she most needed it and ensured she was registered in time for the King's visit, he'd told her about her family and how they'd saved her. She felt comfort around Sydare, knowing their parents were best friends, she felt connected and safe.

Before Millewa had even finished saying 'I do,' Sydare thrust her hand into his and jumped, straight into the deep, blue lagoon and sank until the underwater tunnel opened into a wider cavity. Millewa's cheeks were filled with air, her eyes wide in panic, they must've plunged a long way down because when she looked up, there was no sign of any hole or exit.

She knew she could hold her breath for a minute or two and by the looks of the underwater canal they were in, they were more than two minutes away from air. Millewa began to swim, frantically, before realising she had no idea where to go or which way was up.

There was no light down this far and her eyes couldn't adjust to the darkness. She turned to Sydare, feeling his face and gripping his hand tight, she had to get a signal to him that she couldn't breathe for much longer. A gentle stroke on the back of her hand sent shivers down her spine, there was no urgency from Sydare, there was no panicked swimming or any indication that he was going to move at all.

This was it, she was done for. She trusted him and she'd made a grave mistake, he had tricked her into jumping in and now she was going to drown, her body to never be recovered from the depths of the underwater pool.

If Millewa could cry underwater, tears would've been streaming down her face.

In all her haste to get out of there, Millewa realised her thoughts had consumed her and the time had well and truly surpassed two minutes, in fact, Millewa didn't feel the need to breathe air at all. She turned to Sydare, a faint outline of his face now visible due to their extended period in the water. Through the darkness, Millewa could make out a large, white grin that spread from ear to pointy ear of Sydare's face.

Continuing to hold her hand, Sydare's legs started fluttering and he began to slowly propel himself and Millewa forward. She gripped his hand tightly and gracefully flicked her legs back and forth, she didn't want Sydare dragging her through the water and preferred to offer a leg where she could.

Millewa didn't understand why or how they were swimming without needing air, but she tried to enjoy the experience rather than focus on the finer details of basic human necessity.

It was serene and beautiful under the water, the deadly silence that encompassed them had an eerie feel, as if something were lurking in each crevice and shadow. Millewa studied each wall and edge, enjoying the intricate carvings of blue, magenta and green that swirled and looped between one another, creating a pattern so detailed, Millewa believed it had to be carved by an incredibly talented creature.

Distracted by the underwater gallery, Millewa didn't even realise how light it had become. Her eyes must have been slowly adjusting to the new brightness. They were no longer swimming in darkness, fumbling around trying not to swim straight into a cave wall, the water was crystal clear and smelt faintly of fresh pineapple and strawberries.

Millewa opened her mouth slightly, hardly in control of what she was doing, and to her surprise, the water was as sweet as it smelt and she smiled gleefully at Sydare as they started their ascent.

Before she knew it, Millewa's head burst into open air, her lungs filling and retracting as she breathed deeply and slowly, savouring every breath. Even though she had no need to breathe underwater, it was still an incredibly uncomfortable situation and she was grateful to breathe real air once more.

She looked around the strange place they had arrived in. They were still underground, thankfully, not as deeply as they were moments ago. They were in a huge cavern that was filled with streaming sunlight that shone through the roof above. Smooth, slippery rocks surrounded the water's edge, just as they had seen at their first pit stop this morning. The water sparkled periwinkle and lapped at the rocky edge as Sydare lazily made his way to the platform just metres away. Millewa noticed a stone staircase leading upwards out of the cavern and assumed this was their exit, to where, she had no idea.

“That was insane!” Millewa scrambled up the stone and lay flat on her back, gazing at the perfectly blue sky above, the air smelled of grass and tulips, the sweetness made Millewa’s head spin.

“Ha! I’m glad you enjoyed it, I thought you were going to pass out when we first jumped in, I did lose feeling in my hand though from you gripping so tight” Sydare chuckled and turned on his side to face Millewa. “For your first cave swim, you did really well.”

“I nearly *did* pass out” Millewa gave a wry smile “I thought you were trying to drown me, my life flashed before my eyes.”

“I’m glad to see how far your trust extends,” Sydare winked. “I thought this would be a nice, secluded place for us to plan our next move.”

“What do you mean? We’re just travelling to Clara, asking King Finfudune to free the elves and then head home, that’s our plan isn’t it?” Millewa looked at Sydare quizzically, he stared at her in disbelief and shock, his mouth wide open and his eyes blinking slowly, as if she’d just asked what two times two was.

“No Millewa, there is so much more to it than that. There are dangerous creatures in the lands of Apricus, set out by the king to discourage movement between the lands. We elves stick to Dewdrop Springs, wizards stick to Clara and that’s that. Travel between lands is unheard of.” Sydare looked at her sternly “we need a plan Millewa and we need to make sure it’s good, otherwise we may as well –”

Before Sydare could finish his sentence, the still, deeply blue water began to ripple. Millewa stared towards the centre of the pool. Her heart racing, her palms beginning to sweat, Millewa looked at Sydare who's face looked just as concerned as hers.

They were no longer alone and something or someone was about to break the surface.

Chapter Ten

The Most Powerful Creature Emerges

Sparks shot from deep beneath the water's surface, an array of violent purples and greens soaring in every direction, bright reds, yellows and oranges zoomed past their faces, creating a blur of colour in their eyes. If it didn't seem so dangerous, Millewa would have found it stunning. With each water ripple, another spark would fly, sending an intense heat through the cavern, pricking their faces like tiny matches burning on their skin. Explosions of light and colour at the end of each spark, whistled and echoed as booming fireworks filled their ears, as their nostrils singed at the smell of smoke.

A low rumble erupted, sending reverberations through the rocks. In an instant, two small, winged creatures burst from depths of the sapphire pool, screeching and whooping as they began zooming around the open air.

Millewa strained her eyes in order to get a good look at what was causing such a raucous. Whatever she was looking at was as fast as a buzzing bee, as small as an action figurine and as brightly coloured as the flowers outside, their tiny chattering wings clapping and fluttering in quick succession. The minute creatures began to slow, weaving their way through the air towards Sydare and Millewa, doing backflips in the air.

They moved so graciously and effortlessly, Millewa felt jealous of their ability to fly with such ease. As they drew nearer, Millewa smiled, from what she could see, floating towards her were no more than what looked like fairies. Sparkling, shiny, shimmering fairies whose luminescent wings shone brightly beneath the sun's rays. Sydare rolled his eyes.

"Sprites." He said indignantly.

"*They* are Sprites?" Millewa questioned, she remembered the one who healed her hand when she first arrived in Dewdrop Springs and burned it. These creatures looked smaller and more mischievous than the Sprites she had come across in her time.

"Yep, they are..." Sydare was cut off.

"– The greatest creature to ever grace this Earth?" the male Sprite chimed in, his garments laden with rich purple and bright greens. His eyes were fiercely emerald, complimenting his frayed shorts and t-shirt, his hair as white as snow.

"Or perhaps, the *most* powerful and loved across all the lands?" this comment came from the female Sprite who's jagged skirt was adorned with red, yellow and orange strips. Her short, curled hair was an intensely red pixie cut, the small freckles across her face dotted in perfect markings.

"Don't flatter yourselves. If you don't mind, we were here

first, so feel free to leave us alone" Sydare scoffed in their direction. Millewa had never seen Sydare so upset over anything before, but these Sprites seemed to be getting on every nerve he had.

"That's rich coming from a trespassing elf. Don't forget this is *our* watering hole. You best count your lucky stars we haven't already attacked" the sprite of green and purple sneered.

Millewa shuffled where she sat, if this truly was their watering hole, she didn't want to stay any longer in fear of being attacked. She'd already seen the kind of magic they could produce and did not wish to know more if it meant getting hurt.

"Pfft" Sydare laughed. "Yeah? What are you puny sprites going to do about it? No one owns this cave and you know it."

The air went tense and everything was silent. Millewa looked from Sydare, to the sprites and back again, trying to gauge what everyone's next move was. She didn't know whether to stand her ground or to run and hide under the nearest rock. Should she just dive straight into the water and hope for the best? Could she hold her breath for another half an hour until it was all over? Her heart began beating out of her chest, water welling and stinging her eyes as she fought back tears.

"You know us sprites are one of the most magical creatures of these lands," the red headed sprite boomed. Her face turning as red as her hair as she stared straight into Sydare's soul, her amber eyes piercing. As quickly as she had angered, she calmed, her gritted teeth now formed a serene smile. "We have far more magic than you elves could ever dream of. We have the ability to heal every creature with a few chants and tinctures, we can make anything, from shined shoes and clothes to tasty treats and pastries but most of all, and most importantly, we can do things wizards can't."

"Yes, well, where that may be true on most counts," Sydare retorted, "in any case, it does not you give you the right to intrude. As I asked before, could you please give us some privacy."

"Not a chance," the purple sprite laughed "we heard what you two were talking about before *someone* so rudely interrupted." He looked towards the female sprite with his eyebrows raised.

"That may be true, but surely you two have no interest in our holiday plans? We are visiting the Crystal Creek, Millewa here has never seen it" Sydare nodded quietly. His voice was calm and completely unlike Sydare. His head was held high and his nose pointed towards the sky, giving an air of prestige.

"Bollocks." The male sprite snorted. "You my friend, are going to see King Finfudune in all his glory and try to denounce his Kingship, all the while requesting the elves be freed from his reign. Or have I missed something?" Sydare stared at the sprite, disbelief shielding his eyes as he attempted to stammer a reply, but words failed him.

"I think that's confirmation Phlox," the red head said. "Don't look so shocked though, we're not here to dob you in, we're here to help."

"What do you mean?" Millewa braced herself as she chimed in, the sprites were only small but had already instilled fear inside Millewa. The red sprite shifted her gaze to Millewa and smiled sweetly.

"Well, you see, you folk aren't the only ones who are oppressed by the King. Us sprites were really given the raw end of the stick when Finfudune began his takeover. We were once equal across the lands and now, we're treated like specks of dirt." She dipped her head and sighed. "I'm not being conceited when I say sprites are the most powerful being, because of our size, Finfudune has captured us and used our powers for slave work and fuelling his own agenda. Your hair would curl if you knew what we'd been put through, recently in particular."

"I'd love nothing more than for you to help, it would be an honour to work alongside you," Millewa said this and genuinely meant it, she had already seen how effortlessly sprites performed magic, she wasn't going to pass this opportunity up.

"Absolutely not" Sydare stood up, his arms folded and tucked under his arms, his shoulders broad and standoffish. "If you think I'm going to have some puny and pathetic sprites accompany us on this trek, you've got another think coming."

With a flick of his wrist, the sprite called Phlox sent fireworks shooting from the ends of his hands, purple and green sparks showered them in a spitting rage. The red head, whose name Millewa did not yet know, contorted her hands in a circular motion, directing her gaze at Sydare, within seconds, he was bound by the hands and ankles struggling against the invisible ropes that now restrained him. His face twisting with fury, his beautiful yellow eyes darkened and bulged as he writhed on the rock trying to escape. Phlox turned his attention to the pool behind them, swooping his arms upwards swiftly, with it, a pouring cascade of blue hued water spilled over the rocky edges, lapping at their ankles as he wrenched the water every which way, fully controlling the liquid with a few fluid motions.

"You see Sydare Jones" Phlox turned to face Sydare as he swirled the pools water mesmerizingly "we may be puny and some may even say we're pathetic, but let there be no doubt in your mind of how capable and controlled we sprites are." With that, he dropped the water, a splatter of droplets splashing their faces.

The red head unlocked her stare and performed a cutting motion, as quickly as she had bound him, Sydare was free and his limbs were untangled. He rubbed his wrists and ankles, a defeated look across his face as he bowed his head to his knees.

"Now that the formalities are over, I'm Phlox, nice to meet you!" Phlox gave a cheerful smile and outstretched his hand to Millewa.

"And I'm Bee-Balm. Bee for short though," the red sprite smiled. "We already know Sydare from town, but we haven't met you yet!"

"I'm Millewa, Millewa Cornell" a gasp erupted from Bee's mouth, her eyes filling with tears. Phlox stared at her, open mouthed, unblinking.

"You... You're Fenwick's long lost daughter?" Bee clasped her hands together and rejoiced. "I can't believe it's really you! Your father was a great man, I mean, a *really* great man. He was a friend to all and an exceptional leader, he ensured equality across these lands and did a lot for the sprites in times of trial. I can see already, Millewa, we are going to be great friends." Bee's ears twitched with excitement as she grabbed Millewa's hands.

Sydare looked loathingly at Phlox and Bee, a long look of disgust as his lip curled into a snarl. Millewa turned to him, frowning at him with confusion as he flicked his face from angry to neutral. Millewa patted him on the shoulder and gave him a long, hard look. She had seen many sides to Sydare since he captured her all those weeks ago, but she had not yet seen this side. This side of him was scary, unrelenting and mean and she knew that she couldn't trust what he would do if he stayed in that mood. She pinned it down to jealousy, jealousy of Millewa forming new friendships and flourishing in a world that she had only recently become accustomed to.

She smiled at Sydare and grabbed his hand. They walked towards the cavern exit and began the long trek back to Dewdrop Springs. If they needed to be as prepared as Sydare said, they would need weapons. And lots of them.

"You'll let them come with us won't you?" Millewa whispered as they walked side by side in the thick brush.

"If they must." Sydare grumbled begrudgingly and walked

quickly ahead. When Millewa tried to continue the conversation, her words fell upon deaf ears as Sydare ignored her until daylight.

Chapter Eleven

Power of None

A heavy thud awoke Millewa from her deep slumber, the bed bouncing with the weight. Millewa's eyes popped open, sunlight streaming through her now open window, the curtains being wrenched back with such ferocity, it startled her. Sydare stood, sheepishly by the curtains waiting for Millewa to say something.

"I'm going to get straight to the point, Millewa," Sydare's body shifted uncomfortably and he moved towards her bed and sat down, the bed bouncing with the extra weight. "I have concerns over those fairies coming with us."

"Sprites." Millewa corrected.

"Yes, yes, wings, small, annoying. Practically the same thing," Sydare waved his hand in dismissal.

"Except... they're not the same thing. Anyways, what point are you getting straight to?" Millewa pressed on.

"Phlox and Bee. I don't know if it's the smartest decision having them come with us. Their wings flutter really loudly, we won't be inconspicuous at all, they'll have to walk, but they won't keep up because they're so small. Essentially they're going to be more of a hindrance than help. You and I are capable of handling this trip alone." Sydare slumped against the wall, sighing deeply as he looked to Millewa's face for reassurance, or a sign that she was going to agree with everything he said.

Millewa gave nothing away. She considered Sydare for a moment, mulling over in her mind why Sydare may have such a big issue with the Sprites and she couldn't pin point what the problem was. She straightened in her bed, took a deep breath and looked into his bright, yellow eyes.

"I think you're being a bit dramatic," she began, quickly realising she'd said the wrong thing, Sydare twisted his face and looked extremely hurt by the comment. His shoulders sagged and his lip drooped, his bright eyes dulling by the second.

"What I mean is, I don't think they're as bad as you think they are. Did you not see their magic yesterday? Imagine how helpful they could be! Their small stature means they can hide in small places and eavesdrop on conversations we won't be able to get to. Their powerful magic will mean we are protected where we go, especially because I have none.

"The more magic we can harness, the better. Who cares if their wings flutter, sometimes walking in the dead silence creeps me out, a bit of background noise eliminates that." Millewa sighed deeply, falling back into her plush arm chair, slumping with her feet splayed, her hands pressed hard against her temples.

"Okay, okay you're right. I'm probably overreacting. But

don't say you don't have any magic, because you would" Sydare straightened himself. "All elves are born with magical properties."

"Even elves who have lived in the human world most of their life?" Millewa questioned.

"Yes. Even those elves. You just need some guidance and help to find out what they are, and I can help with that." He smiled sweetly at her, Millewa could tell by the look on his face he genuinely wanted to help. Who was she to say no to that? "You see, all elves are born to a powerful element, whether it be wind, water, earth, or fire and all their magic surrounds that element. As young elves we are provided with training in order to control the element, harness its power and use it for good, not evil."

"Well, what do you think mine could be?" Millewa's head was spinning like a thousand whirlwinds, nothing in her being had ever eluded to power or magic. She really, truly believed she was born a dud, with nothing special or fantastical about her.

"Let's go find out." Sydare tugged at Millewa's arm and pulled her from the room.

Millewa was pulsating with nerves, would she truly find out what her powers were today? What would her element be? She couldn't contain her excitement or concern, so much so, she emptied the contents of her stomach on the front lawn of Sydare's house, feeling better for doing so, she wiped her mouth and continued walking. Sydare promptly provided her with a handful of mint leaves to help cleanse her mouth.

Sydare lead Millewa through the town, waving and smiling as they passed familiar and unfamiliar faces of sprites and elves of all ages. Some were travelling from the market, wicker baskets in hand, fresh vegetables neatly stacked within. Others were younger, walking and skipping, chatting excitedly as they headed to their morning classes. Millewa and Sydare were too old to partake in schooling anymore. Millewa had asked Sydare in the first week about her obligations, he promptly told her that most elves graduate by the time they are fourteen, only the really stupid ones stay any longer. She was glad to know she wasn't too foolish.

Millewa smiled to herself as a young elf, slightly shorter than her, chased a huge Monarch butterfly through the centre of town, giggling and grinning from ear to ear. Millewa was reminded of sweet Remy who used to sit next to her on the bus. A twang of pain in her chest, though she may not admit it. She surely was missing home.

Millewa walked briskly behind Sydare until they hit a set of straight, towering trees that formed a barrier on the outer edge of Dewdrop Springs. Millewa had been here before, when she had followed Sydare sneakily to his combat training. For her sake and his, she had to pretend she had never seen it before. She stepped through the threshold warily, large, brown leaves crunching beneath her boots. Once across the main part of the clearing, Sydare swung on his heel and faced Millewa, hands by his sides, head high, eyes unblinking. A military stance.

"Are you ready to be tested, elf?" Sydare's body didn't move, his head kept at an incline, his yellow eyes staring straight ahead. Millewa shuffled uncomfortably.

"Uh, sure" she looked around nervously and waited.

Sydare circled Millewa, like a shark circling its prey in the water. He kept an unusually close distance and stared unwavering at her.

"Perfect," he uttered after a few seconds "we shall begin with water, my personal favourite, as it is the element I align with."

Sydare took a few steps back. He made a circular motion with his hands repeatedly, drawing an invisible circle in the air.

"Try this," Sydare now motioned to Millewa to give it a go. For now, his hands were filled with clear, sparkling water that bubbled and swayed in the sunlight. Millewa began motioning her hands in the same way, subtle, smooth movements in order to conjure a water circle. But it was to no avail. No matter how quickly, slowly, calmly or manic she tried. There was no water spouting from her.

"Well. I guess water isn't my thing" she shrugged, slightly defeated, but also slightly glad her power would differ from Sydare's.

"No, no" Sydare started "element conjuring is super advanced, I would've been shocked if you had got it on your first go. Here, let me test your ability to withstand the elements. If you are unable to withstand water, you'll surely drown."

"Great." Millewa said sarcastically.

"I won't let that happen! Don't you worry your blonde elven head." With his hands he twisted an invisible sphere, using his fingers to stretch and pull, contracting at regular intervals. With a massive heave of force, Sydare pushed outwards towards the open clearing, sending an almighty jet from his hands cascading onto the luscious grass.

It didn't take long for the area to flood, and not just any kind of flood, but a Noah's Ark scale flood, or so Millewa thought. They were surrounded by water, as if they were in a huge underwater dome, she could see the outside world around them, moving and living within the air. Birds were flying above, small animals were grazing by the trees and Millewa was breathing just fine in her bubble of water!

She began jumping with glee, water was *her* element too, she turned to Sydare, giving him a big thumbs up of success.

Sydare simply shook his head and swiftly pointed at his hand that was grasping Millewa's elbow, allowing her to breathe under water as it had done so before. Sydare shared a wry smile, motioning his right arm in a swirling motion. As quick as the water had come, it was gone and once again they were standing on dry land, breathing air.

"I'm sorry," Sydare offered, eyes gazing deeply at Millewa. She could tell he wanted to say more but didn't quite have the words for her. "If it's any consolation, there are still three more elements to try, this was only the first one. It would have been pretty incredible to have the same one though."

"What's next then?" Millewa asked, picking at her nails nervously, awaiting what test may lie ahead for her.

"Wind." Sydare said bluntly, adding "also known as the weather element. Controller of temperature, air speeds and storms. If I had the choice of which element to align with, it would be wind. I've always been envious of those in control of the weather."

"If you aren't aligned, then how will you test me?" Millewa asked shortly. "Water is your element so obviously you're able to test my strength and weakness, but you've got no attachment to wind."

"The old fashioned elven testing drills used big machines. Now they're a little more streamlined with this," Sydare held up what looked like a TV remote.

A small, rectangular device that had various buttons on it. A windy day symbol, a water droplet, a tree and a red flame. Each symbol had a little dial attached to it with the words 'min' and 'max' on either side. Though simple, Millewa knew it must hold some great power. Her insides churned as she prepared for the next test.

Millewa stood completely still as Sydare clicked the 'windy day' button on his remote, he hovered over the dial before increasing it slightly from the minimum. Without warning, the sky around them darkened, the clouds a dark charcoal, shadows cast down from the sky, caressing every inch in darkness. A cool wind whistled past Millewa's ears and she looked to Sydare for guidance. What was she to do with a black sky?

"You need to harness the storm!" Sydare shouted over the now roaring wind, his knotted hair flailing, whipping his face in quick succession.

"But how?!" Millewa shouted back, beginning to panic. Bolts of lightning and shocks of thunder reverberated through her body, the storm growing wilder with each breath she took.

Millewa's eyes were manic.

She put her hands out in front of her, willing the storm to cease, giving every fibre of her being over to the storm, allowing it to encase her as she begged for it to stop. Harsh, wheezing wind pierced her ears and stung her eyes.

Millewa threw out her hands, leaning back with her chest to the sky, screaming with all her mite for it to stop. She stomped her feet aggressively to the ground, when the lightning from above, struck her right in the heart.

Millewa collapsed and the world around her went black.

"Millewa, *Millewa*" Sydare whispered in her ear as she jolted awake, eyes dazed and her brain a blurry mess.

She forced herself to blink, to see the clear sky above and the sun shining through the clouds, to hear the soft whistling of the wind. There was no storm, no fierceness to fear, the clearing was as it was before Sydare clicked that button. After a few short minutes, Millewa's vision was completely cleared and she felt one hundred percent herself again.

“How is it I feel so fine after being struck by lightning? Does that mean wind is my power?” Millewa looked hopefully at Sydare, her gaze met by a shameful glance that didn’t give her much hope.

“You see, I had the dial turned to max when the brute force of the storm hit you” Sydare’s smiled faded from his face.

“YOU WHAT?” Millewa felt her face burning with rage, her pointed ears standing on edge, wiggling with disgust and her bright blue eyes turned a dull shade of grey.

“I had a bet with Dad, that your power would align with wind. I thought you’d handle it, but when I heard you scream in a fit of pain, I turned the dial right down to min. That was when the lightning struck you. If the dial had been at max you would’ve died, but because it had been toned back, you were only knocked out.” Sydare shuffled his feet and sighed “I’m sorry.”

“You are so darn lucky I didn’t die. Otherwise I’d have to haunt you forever!” Millewa outstretched her hand, reaching for Sydare to help her up. “What element are we testing next?”

“You really want to go again so soon?” Sydare’s eyes brightened. He was impressed with her bravery.

“Definitely.” Millewa smirked.

Sydare once again picked up the controlling device. He pondered it for a moment before deciding which element to choose, his slender fingers hovering over the buttons before decidedly landing on earth.

“Now the earth element is quite pleasant,” Sydare encouraged.

"With the element of earth, you can grow fresh food at an incredible rate and it'll be the most delicious thing you'll ever taste. You can sprout the housing trees without a worry, creating homes for those in need. Best of all, you can burrow underground, weaving and carving monstrous caverns, that can certainly come in handy." Millewa liked the idea of the earth element, she had always loved outside and the smell of grass and greenery. This surely had to be her element. "The best part of testing earth, is it is completely painless, there's no risk of death."

Millewa took her place next to Sydare, waiting for him to once again flip the switch. Her heart fluttering with nerves and excitement. This process so far had been terrifyingly terrific, the rush of adrenaline when she cheated death, the intense extremes of the elements. She could barely wait for what earth had in store for her. No sooner had the thought left her mind when the flat grounds around them began to change.

Solid mounds began sprouting from below their feet and cascading hills were soon all they could see. Millewa looked to Sydare, unsure of what the test required of her, he simply smiled back at her, giving her a big thumbs up as if that helped her decipher what she needed to do.

She stared at the wide expanse of land, willing herself to take it all in. There was no rush, Sydare said there was no risk of death so she could take in the scenery for a minute. Greens of every shade dotted the land below them, soft grass shoots tickling their toes. A sweet, delectable smell filled the air.

Millewa closed her eyes and took a long, deep breath, feeling the sun on her face, the warmth flooding her cheeks. She felt blissfully happy and calm, maybe this was the effect of the earth element alignment, with this Millewa opened her eyes.

A sudden urge, an overwhelming feeling of power, Millewa placed her hands out in front of her and began twisting and sweeping, her arms contorting in a fluid motion. A continued surge. She felt the power in her finger tips.

This was it.

Millewa continued to sweep and swish, her eyes bright with excitement.

"Concentrate. Concentrate." Sydare began coaxing Millewa, his hand outstretched, as if telling her to stop. "Keep focus, don't stop." Millewa stared intently at the hills, willing them to part, giving her all to split them and tunnel. But nothing came. Before too long, Millewa's head was pounding from the intensity, her arms beginning to cramp, her eyes watering. Earth wasn't her element and she slumped to the floor in defeat. A swift click of the button and the hills receded, leaving them once again in the flat, boring clearing.

"I really thought that was the one," Millewa conceded to Sydare, "The warmth of the air, the grass between my toes and the wind ruffling my hair. I really *felt* it."

"I'm sorry." Sydare attempted to hug Millewa, she stepped back in lieu of his pity "at least we know your fire test will be straight forward. It's the only element left."

"Let's get it over with then." Millewa sighed.

Sydare grasped the remote for the final time. Millewa could see his hands shaking, he was nervous, maybe more so than Millewa. His fingers lingered for a moment over the switch and dial, his eyes concentrated, furrowing his brow into a deep frown, the lines in his forehead creasing with growing intent.

Flick. The air changed. The clouds above them darkened. And a hot wind began to rip through clearing. The sky was red, the trees surrounding them became a deep crimson, flickering and dancing in the wind, beautiful but menacing all at the same time.

Millewa stared closely, allowing the hot air to take over her senses, she felt an overwhelming pulse of fear. The trees weren't glowing from the reflection; they were on fire. Hot, dangerous flames licked the edge of the clearing, engulfing the greenery into fiery balls of rage. The rhythmic movement almost mesmerising as they swayed like the long grassy fields near Millewa's human home.

Millewa blinked. She had to snap out of the trance. To control fire, she would need to contain it, stop the spread and move the flames in whichever direction she wished. She knew the elves with fire, they were strong, powerful and determined. This was not how she saw herself, but it was the only element left. It had to work.

Millewa raised her hands in front of her face, elongating her fingers in a slender motion. The fire crackled behind her eyes as she attempted to shift the flame with her mind.

A huge roar of wind nearly knocked her to the ground, a sudden shock thundering through the ground, a crack forming in the centre of the clearing. Deep, surging gurgles erupted from the core, bubbling and frothing at the edge.

Lava.

Why did Millewa not consider lava, possibly one of the deadliest and dangerous parts of fire that was now toppling over the edge and heading their way. She had to control it, had to seize it so they may survive. Being burnt alive was not how she wanted to go, nor did she want to risk Sydare. All her focus and attention was at the boiling liquid that was now spilling towards them, forming a catastrophic river.

"C'mon Millewa, you've got this. Take control. Change its direction." There was nervousness in Sydare's voice, he was scared. So was Millewa. The oozing magma showing no signs of slowing as it burnt the grassy path to a crisp.

Focus. *Focus.* The lava was now metres away from her toes, she could feel the heat radiate, burning her face like a dog's hot breath.

She felt faint again, as if all the moisture in her body had been sucked out and into the lava. She couldn't control it, it was too powerful, too hot, too much for one elf to handle. Her eyes became heavy, her knees weak at the wall of heat. This was it.

Her body crumpled to the floor, her mind foggy, she waited for the lava to swallow her whole. But it never came. In fact, the heat disappeared altogether and she was curled, shaking and breathless when she met Sydare's yellow eyes.

"I had to call it. It couldn't have gone any longer without killing us both." A sad, pitied look stung Millewa like a wasp. She had nothing. No element. No power.

"So that's it then?" She could feel tears welling behind her eyes and tried to force them back. She had never felt disappointment like this before. "I have no power?"

"I can't believe it either, there hasn't been a powerless elf born in centuries. Your parents were two of the most powerful I knew. I'm a little lost for words, Millewa." There it was again. Pity.

"It must be from living with the humans for all those years, maybe their normality wore off on me. Plus, my parents are dead, maybe my magic died with them. Anyways, Where do we go from here?" Millewa tried to distract herself from the reality of the situation, forcing her mind to think of anything else.

"I guess that's a very real possibility." Sydare slumped where he stood, his shoulders sagging at what he was about to say "I'm not powerful enough to help us both. So, I also guess this means we *do* need the sprites to accompany us."

Millewa smiled broadly, "I thought you'd never say yes."

Chapter Twelve

Eagle Landing

Millewa slept with the blinds open through the night. She was restless and spent most of the night gazing at the cloudless sky, stars twinkled against the inky black. Tomorrow they would leave for Clara and in a few days' time they would confront The Wizard King. Life as she knew it was about to change, for better or for worse.

She rolled in her bed, feeling the soft, fluffy texture of her blanket. She snuggled in, closing her eyes and willing sleep to take over. Before too long, she fell into a deep, dreamless sleep.

The morning breeze kissed Millewa's cheeks, the briskness stinging her nose slightly as it wrinkled with discomfort. Millewa opened her eyes, expecting a harsh light to hit her, instead she was delighted to see a buttery, pink hued sky streaming in the open frame.

Calm before the storm, she thought wistfully. She stretched every limb, feeling the relief wash over her, when Sydare knocked on the door and let himself into the room. They were silent for a moment, both accepting the magnitude of what they were about to embark on.

Millewa's ears pricked up, she could hear a whistling sound just outside her window, flapping and twizzling filled the air. Confused and a bit afraid, Millewa walked towards the window, looking down to see what was making the racket.

ZOOM!

One tiny, red and orange spark zipped past her nose. *Zoom, zoom!* Another tiny spark. This time it was violent purple and dashing green, chattering all around her head. Millewa couldn't turn her head quick enough to catch a good look at the creature. Instead all she saw was a blur of colour and light, tricking her eyes and confusing her senses.

"Phlox and Bee," Sydare said irritably "Must you enter in such chaos?" Sydare wasn't pleased the sprites had entered his house so abruptly, and he certainly wasn't ready for their presence so early in the morning.

"Oh come on, this is exactly what we were saying yesterday wasn't it?" Millewa interrupted "Their power is incredible, they reached the window ledge in a matter of seconds!" Sydare's face twisted into pure distaste.

Phlox flew right up to Sydare's face, wings fluttering loudly, clicking as if to say '*ha, ha*'. Phlox raised his hands to his head, as if making moose antlers at his temples, twinkled his fingers and stuck his tongue out as far as he could, blowing the biggest raspberry in Sydare's face. Sydare swiped his hand out, trying to catch the sprite in his fingers, alas, Phlox was too quick and continued to buzz around his head, throwing taunts and insults.

Millewa and Bee watched with embarrassment, both boys were being foolish and the girls couldn't stand it!

"Alright enough!" Millewa finally shouted over the raucous behaviour. "Honestly, that's enough! If we're all going to go on this trip together, we *need* to get along with one another." Sydare and Phlox exchanged disgusted looks.

"We're not saying you need to be best friends" added Bee.

"Exactly, you just need to tolerate one another enough for us to complete our mission." Millewa agreed. "We've got a long way to go, and what sort of message does it send to The King about harmony and equality, when you two can't gather yourselves for even two minutes without going at one another's throats?"

"We're sorry," both Sydare and Phlox added in unison.

"That's fine, now we have far more important things to worry about. We leave today and we need to make sure we are one hundred percent prepared for what lays ahead." Millewa shuffled around under her bed, looking for paper she had scribbled on the night before "Ah! Here it is. *Ahem.* I wrote a list before I went to bed last night of what we need and who's gathering it. Phlox and Bee, you're in charge of food and drinks. I'm taking control of the comfort side and packing our tents. And Sydare, you're in charge of defence and weapons. We need to be efficient, we don't have time for foolery. Meet at the front gate of the house in one hour."

They all nodded in agreement. Knowing their roles, they split up. Phlox and Bee whipped out the window, Sydare smiled and raced down the hall.

Millewa, left to herself, got dressed in her most comfortable travelling clothes, a singlet with a light, grey knit jumper, flowy, brown corded pants and thick soled boots that were soft as clouds to walk in. She bunched her hair into a low bun, clipping back the front where it dangled, smoothing out her part. She was ready to begin packing.

It was hard to know where to begin, if all went well, they would only be gone a few days and would need minimal resources. If things went terribly wrong, they could be gone for weeks.

Millewa had pulled two large travel bags from her cupboard, made of moleskin and leather, they should keep out most weather elements. She laid them on the ground, awaiting her arrival when she returned with supplies, and snuck down the stairs into the front garden where Alvie was pruning his fruit trees. A small gasp escaped Millewa's mouth, not wanting to be seen by Alvie she jumped into the nearest bush. She didn't have time to waste, nor could she wait for Alvie to leave the garden, he often spent hours outside tending to his vegetables, she needed to make a move now.

Keeping low and calm, Millewa army crawled under the back row of bushes, dirt flicking into her eyes, causing them to water.

She was thankful Alvie hadn't yet watered the plants, or she would be trudging through mud right now. Before exiting the shelter of the mulberry bush, she checked to see where Alvie was.

Humming merrily, playing very close attention to his apple tree, Millewa found her chance to duck from the bushes and slip out the side gate, hunching over as she ran towards the main street, determined not to be seen. Once she found the safety of the cobblestones, she straightened, took a deep breath and continued her walk into town.

Sydare had given Millewa all of his pocket money to buy their supplies. Sixteen gold dollars and sixty-three silver cents jangled in her pockets, weighing down the right side of her pants.

Sydare had explained the monetary process to her days earlier, ensuring she understood how to pay for things in town. Gold dollars were rich in monetary value and there are nine silver cents to every gold dollar. Millewa cursed her maths teacher for not drilling their nine times tables, her mathematical thinking was below dismal. She would need to use her fingers to calculate how many gold dollars her silver cents were worth.

Her first stop was the *Outdoorsmans' Plantation.* The store resides behind the main strip of shops, down an uneven alley with all sorts of unusual activity stores.

On the right, there was the *Fish Hook Inn*, which provided refreshments and ales to the local tenders and accommodation and meals for out of towners.

The Bee Sting was a store that specialised in all things bees.

Selling bees for hives, using bee sting venom to create soaps, gels and oils to help with muscular pain and the most delicious, creamy honey that you will ever taste. *The Bee Sting* was incredibly popular for food store owners, as most of their sweet treats included *The Bee Sting* honey. There was a rumour that *The Bee Sting* also sold venom to the black market, profiting off weapons and dark items being made from the bees, but Millewa knew no truth to this.

The final store on the right was *Wood Works*, fine wooden furnishings were made and sold from the one shop, highly expensive and rarely bought, *Wood Works* only needed one sale a fortnight to make a profit.

The left of the street was much brighter. The first, was one of Millewa's absolute favourites *So-Damn-Fizzy*. The store was incredibly colourful, loud pop music played out the open, white-framed windows, where the whole back wall of the shop was laden with cordials of every flavour, butterscotch, limeade and cola were some of the regular choices. Vegemite, chestnut and marshmallow were a few of the more outrageous options. You simply pick your flavour, pick your fizz level from one to five, and choose the size of your glass bottle (small, medium, large or super large), then the clerk would mix it up right in front of you, cap it and send you on your way for only two silver cents!

Next door was where Millewa was headed; *Outdoorsmans' Plantation – for all your adventuring needs!* The store was so large it took the space of the final two plots.

The shop front was exquisitely painted. Beautiful, detailed trees wrapped around the edges of windows and doors, vines twisted amongst the throng of stumps and branches, every shade of green cuddled one another in a splatter of leaves. The tree trunks were chocolate brown with deep indents, mimicking the grain of wood. Each window was painted in deep sea blue and the wooden doors were stained in a rich, red tint. The final touch to the mesmerising shop front were the door knobs. Gold plated, placed on each side of the wide double door entry, an eagle superbly carved into it.

Millewa stared at the eagle and she could've sworn one gave her a small wink. But that would be nonsense.

Although she loved visiting, she had never even been in the store, just admired the beauty from the street. She clicked out of her daydream, after the charade of dodging Alvie this morning, she was running low on time to get the resources they needed.

Millewa gave a solid push on the door, it creaked and moaned as it swung open to the dimly lit shop.

"Ah, good morning, at last we meet" a squat elf with wild, grey hair emerged from behind the front desk, covered in what looked like dirt and bread crumbs. "I see you pass by my shop often and I am pleased you finally decided to come in." Millewa smiled awkwardly, she was embarrassed that the shop owner had watched her stare.

She turned her head around the shop. It was huge and contained every sort of camping gear you could ever need. Rows of tents with all abilities; small and compact, extremely lightweight, house-sized, you name it, they had it. Drinking canisters that folded to no more than a drink bottle lid, backpacks that were fully equipped with hunting gear, sun protection and sleepwear, a real all in one product.

Millewa gawked at how much there was and became instantly overwhelmed at how she was going to buy their gear so quickly without getting it wrong.

"That, is where I come in." Millewa jolted, did, did the shop owner just read her thoughts? "Yes indeed I did, I'm Rowena Durward the owner and operator of *Outdoorsmans' Plantation*, but I am also a talented diviner, so it makes it very simple to help my customers find exactly what they need. What exactly do you *think* you need? Millewa went blank and panicked. *Don't think about The Wizard King, don't think about the confrontation, don't...*

"Wizard King, hey? Well, sounds like you have a long trip ahead of you, you'll need an all-inclusive tent. Built in beds, doonas, pillows. The works." Rowena smiled, she was clearly impressed with her own gift and didn't mind showing it off.

"That would be wonderful thank you." Millewa replied.

"You may also need these," Rowena passed Millewa a handful of colourful beans, all with strange markings and patterns. "You know; you can never be too careful on such a treacherous trek. All you need to do, if in danger, is throw a bean at the ground and watch the marvel take place. But that is all I'll say about that."

"How rough is the journey? And thank you, by the way," Millewa placed the beans in the top pocket of her shirt, they seemed to buzz with electricity.

"It is tough, but it's the monsters you encounter along the way that really test you." Rowena's face turned grave, she stared at her shoes with a grim smile. "Anywho, take this, on the house of course for, um, luck." Rowena placed a golden badge in Millewa's hand, an eagle, the same as on the door knob was pressed and carved into the gold.

"Wow. You really are too kind." Millewa pressed the curves into her fingers, feeling the cool edges, strangely she felt a connection and curiosity towards it, but she couldn't figure out why.

After more perusing and mind reading from Rowena, Millewa eventually left with her pockets considerably lighter than when she had come, and her hands much fuller. Twist top water bottles, all-inclusive tents, fire starters, pillow popper cushions for sitting outdoors and a thick, woollen mat that would act as their flooring for the next little while. Rowena even threw in firefly crackers for free. Small, luminescent bugs that when you flick their behinds, light up like a lamp.

Millewa rushed from the shop quickly, ran through the back street to the main square, all the way to Sydare's house. She stopped only once she had dumped all her shopping bags on her bedroom floor, falling onto her bed, puffing with exhaustion.

"How did it all go?" Sydare stood - weaponry hanging off him - in Millewa's doorway. He had clearly been far more productive than she had.

"Good. Except that shopkeeper is quite strange, did you know she can-"

"Read minds? Yeah I did, I probably should've warned you about that. Rowena is brilliant, but also very nosy." Sydare shrugged as if this was a common occurrence with Rowena.

"She also gave me these" Millewa outstretched her hands, the beans and pin scattered across her palms.

Sydare gaped, "She gave you that pin? For free?"

"Ah yeah, is it valuable or something?" Millewa turned her head to the side, the pin wasn't new, nor was it really old, it honestly looked like something she might've pulled from her human cereal boxes.

"Let me take a closer look," Sydare's demeanour changed as he turned the pin over in his hands. "Actually, from closer inspection, no it's nothing special. Probably some voodoo mind reading stuff. I'd toss it if I were you." Millewa couldn't deny the pulse she felt in her hands when holding it though, and decided against Sydare's advice.

"Where are Phlox and Bee?" Millewa quickly changed the subject.

"I passed them not too long ago in the garden, they're harvesting a few things from out the front. We'll just pack these into the bags and meet them down there." Sydare held out the weapons, as if Millewa could magically make them shrink to fit in their backpacks.

Without a second thought, Sydare had tossed them slightly in the air and they disappeared. Or so she thought. In Sydare's palms were tiny, miniature versions of the bows, spears and shields Sydare had decorated himself with. With a wry smile, he dropped them in to a pocket in their bags and headed towards the front door.

Millewa followed, she was surprised at how light the backpacks were considering how much they had crammed into them. Just as they arrived at the pulley system to the yard, a call came from over her shoulder.

"A word before you go, Millewa" Alvie sat in the big, squishy arm chair, mesmerised by the fire crackling in the wall. Millewa's heart sank and a sick feeling began rising in her chest, the acidity burning her throat. "I saw sprites in my house this morning."

"Phlox and Bee, they're our friends" Millewa realised Alvie hadn't asked a question.

"Interesting. Where are you going with these sprites? I see your bags are packed for more than just a day trip. I also notice your friends ruffling through my vegetable garden." Millewa gulped. The sick feeling continued to bubble.

"Well, we enjoyed camping so much the other day we decided we'd take Phlox and Bee this time. You know, a bit further out. We'll be gone four days" Millewa gave a pained grin, trying to sound light hearted.

"Four days? That's about enough time to get to Clara and back, isn't it?" Sprung. They were doomed now.

"Is it?" Millewa played dumb, if she pretended she knew nothing, maybe Alvie wouldn't be so harsh.

"Quit pretending Millewa, I could hear you and Sydare talking last night about your grand plan to visit The King." Alvie finally turned to face her.

"No, we weren't, we..." Millewa stammered.

"Don't lie. I'm not angry. But you also need to know what you're getting yourself into. I was best friends with your father and I know better than to try and stop you from leaving. He was stubborn and I'm guessing, so are you." Millewa nodded in agreement, Alvie's face had turned kind, almost pitying. "There are many creatures that lurk beyond the safety of Dewdrop and you should do well to remember that. You'll need an elf flare, I'm assuming Sydare packed one when he raided my weaponry cabinet, but I'd like you to take another just in case." Alvie pulled a box from beneath the couch, filled with tiny defensive and offensive weapons.

"I'm sorry but what *is* an elf flare?" Millewa put her palm out to receive five of the tiny gun shaped items.

"When an elf flare is set off, it sends a signal directly to the parents of the sender. In your case, you reside with us and are our responsibility, so naturally, your flare would alert myself and Berrima." Alvie barely took a breath before he continued on. "You'll also need this, it's a Far Fetch Map. You simply pin point your destination on the map and it'll direct you straight there, a bright, white line will appear on the map, all you have to do is follow it."

"Thanks, Alvie, I really appreciate your help" Millewa hugged him, he had been nothing but kind since she arrived and she truly was grateful for all they'd done. She headed for the pulley system when she was once again called back.

"One more thing before you go. Remember what's at stake when you take this journey on. Your decisions affect not only yourself but all of elf kind. By taking this on, you put everyone at risk. Your actions could cause a war and you need to be aware that you are completely liable for what happens from this point forward." Alvie gave her a stern look before turning back to the fire as it roared in agreement.

Millewa slowly lowered herself down the pulley. Guilt and worry overcoming her senses as she made the descent to the yard. If she was the cause of a war, should she really be pushing the most powerful being in the land?

Then the eagle pin started to buzz.

Chapter Thirteen
The King's Sentry

Millewa's worry must have been written all over her face when she came to the bottom of the tree, as Sydare was straight onto her about what had happened with his dad. As the sprites packed the food into their bags, Millewa began filling Sydare in on what Alvie had lectured her about.

"He worries too much," Sydare said flatly, "I wouldn't worry, he feels some sort of responsibility to Dewdrop since your dad died and he really hasn't adjusted well. I'd forget he said anything at all." Millewa could see Sydare was trying to make her feel better but she couldn't shake what he'd said about a war. Any time her mind slipped towards thinking about war, the eagle pin began ferociously vibrating, almost as if it was excited by the idea.

"Shall we go then?" Bee zipped the back of Millewa's pack and flew to sit on her shoulder. Millewa was grateful for the distraction.

Of all the times Millewa had left their valley, they had

travelled South and stopped at the river before trudging back. This time was different.

A sharp cut across the town square, avoiding eye contact with anyone who bothered to look and they were due East. Their pace quick, almost too quick for Millewa's legs to keep up, but they wanted to be out of town before anyone spotted which direction they were going.

The landscape began to change quickly and drastically. Once through the thick, rough bush, the trees ceased to exist and open, sweeping plains stretched for miles, further than any of their eyes could see. Wind whipping their faces, grass as long as their knees and the smell of strawberries enveloped their noses, making their mouths water instantly.

Millewa had never been in air as fresh as this before, she gulped it in as if she'd never breathed before and wished they could live in this moment forever, instead of going to whatever they were walking into.

The pure silence broke, as Phlox took flight from Sydare's shoulder and buzzed a metre from Millewa's face.

"So, you never filled us in on your power," Phlox pressed, "What is it? Bee and I were taking bets, I thought fire because you are absolutely ruthless and stubborn. Bee thought water because she views you as calming. Stupid thought really."

"I don't have one." Millewa replied flatly.

"What do you mean you don't have one? Every elf gains a power; it's just how development works!" Phlox was shocked and slightly upset.

"From all the training material, she conjured nothing and couldn't control a thing. I've never seen anything like it," Sydare added.

"Yeah right. Strange. Maybe because we all thought you were dead, that's why you didn't develop anything, the magic just faded away when you were declared gone." Phlox looked puzzled, but he also nodded in agreement with what he had just said. "Where were you anyways? And how on earth did you get back here with no magic?"

"That, I can answer. I was in the human world, adopted as a singed baby and raised by two foster parents. Both of whom hate me now. We were on a family holiday near the Ingens Mountain region when I had something – well someone – following me. Sydare captured me not long after and here I stand. Back where I really belong. That's the short version of it all."

"Wow. That is some story. Why'd you try get her back?" Phlox now turned his attention to Sydare.

"As you said, we thought she was dead. Then I smelt her. The family scent was so strong I couldn't believe it. I knew Fenwick and Alma had perished, but there was always so much speculation around Millewa herself. So I tracked, I traced and you best believe I found her walking through the forest alone. That's when I brought her back to her true home. This is where she belongs." Phlox seemed satisfied with this answer, he sat himself back on Sydare's shoulders and didn't say another word.

The sun moved slowly through the sky, the dusty pink hues of the morning settling into powdered blue, dotted with fluffy white clouds. The air not too warm, not too cold, perfect for trekking through stunning fields. Millewa marvelled at the flat, swaying paddocks, so much so she missed the creek that had appeared on their left and the rugged mountain that now lay in before them in the distance.

"I've never seen anything like it before" Millewa exclaimed.

"It's incredible isn't it. We really are lucky to live where we are, The King could've taken all of this from us, but yet we still get to live here."

Sydare smiled to himself, a lot must have happened whilst she was away. "Stick to the creek while walking too, it's the most direct route to Clara." Obediently, Millewa, Phlox and Bee followed.

There was no rush in their steps today, they meandered through the grass as if they had all the time in the world. Everyone was getting along and they'd had a pleasant walk in the wake of all the warnings.

"What's your favourite food then, Millewa?" Bee questioned from a metre behind, "Mine is Beetlejuice and frangipani tarts!" Millewa was slightly perplexed by Bee's sudden interest in her taste buds, but she figured Bee was probably just trying to get to know her.

"You may not have heard of it; human food is *way* different to your elven or sprite food." Millewa walked backwards to make eye contact with her. "It would have to either be Shepherd's Pie or Spaghetti Bolognese. Both are equal on my favourites list."

"Sounds weird." Bee chuckled "Why would a shepherd be in a pie? Gross. Hey, Sydare, what about you? You eat normal food like us!"

"Sh." Sydare snapped. "Stop talking." A whisper.

Sydare crouched low, looking ahead along the river. Millewa crouched behind him, trying to see what he was looking at. There it was. A huge, mountainous dog-like creature, bent over drinking from the creek. Millewa recognised it almost instantly as the savage, rabid animal that Sydare had fought in battlement training. The Amarok. She knew better than to mention that she knew this animal, so she instead asked what it was.

"It's an Amarok," Sydare whispered, barely audible from how low his voice was. "We need to stay quiet and we need not disturb it. They're vicious, cunning animals that will rip your throat out before you even get the chance to scream." Didn't Millewa already know that!

As if it heard their hearts beating out of their chests, The Amarok began to sniff the air. Long, strong sniffs that echoed through the valley in which they stood, it's yellowed eyes searching for the source of the smell. Until it finally looked at them, eyes glaring, teeth menacing, a low grumble reverberated through the earth.

"RUN!" Sydare shouted.

If the Amarok wasn't entirely sure of them before, he

certainly was now, and it was certain now that he didn't want them alive. Huge, booming footsteps pounded toward them, eyes locked to kill. Millewa knew better than to hang around and sprinted towards cover.

Across the valley an enormous tree stood alone, low lying branches enticed Millewa to climb it. Her heart was beating out of her chest as the run and adrenaline caught up with her. She wasted no time in scrambling up the tree and into a safe view point. She could see no one had followed her. Her lack of magic now proving an issue.

Yellow, orange, purple and green sparks showered the Amarok, as small flames licked at the creatures' fur. Phlox and Bee were in full fight mode as they hurtled curse after curse to try and tame it. To no avail, the Amarok charged forward, mouth frothing with pearly white foam. Phlox and Bee had no more to give and were forced to flee towards the tree as well. Wings low and spirits depleted.

It was now up to Sydare to face it alone.

Sydare dropped the bag that hung from his shoulders and with a swift movement of his arms, a shield and spear appeared in either hand. The warrior Millewa had once seen in battle, had returned.

Swift, calculating movements took over Sydare's body. He deflected powerful lunges with his shield and whipped its face with his spear stick. The Amarok didn't seem to slow and it pushed forward onto Sydare. They wrestled to the ground, teeth gnashing menacingly, hoping to bite him in half. Sydare was lost under the streaks of fur and muscle. Millewa felt ill. What would happen if on day one, Sydare was killed? And she had to face Alvie, after he'd told her what was at stake.

A shriek erupted from the Amarok, Sydare, red faced and sweaty climbed on top the beast and stared down into its eyes. It wasn't dead or dying, but in a trance. Staring blankly at Sydare, tongue protruding from its mouth and flopping at its side. He had tamed it. At least enough to walk away without risk of being eaten. He had done it so swiftly, Millewa could've blinked and missed it. Phlox, Bee and Millewa stared, panting and in awe of the fact he didn't walk away with more than a scratch.

"One of The King's outer ground protectors. Nasty things" Sydare called as he walked toward them. "There'll be more, if not worse creatures we'll come across these next few days. Keep your wits about you, and Bee, stop talking so damn loud." Bee shrunk where she sat.

Millewa looked to Sydare, concern spread across her face. She knew she was useless in that battle and if things were going to get worse, who's to say they should fight to protect her?

"It'll be fine," Sydare reassured her. "That may have looked rough, but I know what I'm doing. Just trust me on that." Millewa had seen his training and knew he was more than capable, which may have been what scared her the most.

Tired, they scrambled halfway up the mountain. Their bones aching and feet sore, they found a clearing resting atop the first crest and decided this was the perfect place to rest for the night.

"Don't orcs live here?" Phlox spat at the ground. "Filthy vermin they are."

"They're further East, there's no way they'd stay so close to the kingdom after what happened in Clara all those years ago." Sydare replied.

"Why are the orcs so bad?" Questioned Millewa.

"Not now." Sydare shut her down.

Millewa walked to flattest part of the clearing and threw the tent popper onto the ground. It sprang to life with a loud *pop* and in front of them stood a huge, grey, house-like tent. It would easily fit them all. One by one they piled into the spacious cavity and prepared the evening meal.

The tent was perfect. Two bunk beds on the far side of the area, topped with blankets, pillows and pyjamas laid out ready to go. The kitchen was a single bench for cutting, a sink, a small stovetop and a fridge that hummed with life. Bee packed away their food into the small cupboard beneath the bench.

A fireplace crackled in the corner, keeping the room toasty and warm. It was simple, but by golly was Millewa glad she paid extra for this tent. Everything was here and ready, nothing had to be folded or packed away tomorrow, it would all shrink into the tiny popper piece, ready to reinflate when they needed it.

Dinner was nothing fancy, toasted wattle seed biscuits with fresh smoked trout and lemon cream cheese. Together they sat around the table and ate in silence, they were thankful to eat and rest without a worry of another Amarok.

"What's the real reason you're doing all of this?" Phlox demanded, staring straight at Millewa, "We all nearly died today because of this quest and I really want to make sure it's worth it."

"That's uncalled for" Sydare shot at him.

"That's completely fair." Millewa spoke directly to Phlox and Bee, "I want peace across these lands, right now the lives of elves and sprites alike are being dictated by a wizard who truly doesn't understand the needs or feelings of us and that's what my dad would've wanted. It's his legacy I need to protect and to once again bring forth all the good work he did to keep his people happy. I'm not going to stand back and watch some evil King ruin everything he stood for."

"Brilliant," Phlox smiled. "That's exactly what I was hoping you would say. Us sprites are small and quiet creatures but we too have had enough of all the crap Finfudune has thrown our way. We're slaves. Working in fruit fields for the wizards to have their tea and killing ourselves in the process. If we are too old, we die. If we refuse, our wings are clipped and sold on the black market. It isn't fair to be treated so poorly when our powers are so immense, we shouldn't be bowing down to anything or anyone. When we reach The King, what do we do Millewa?"

"I think we try talk to him, we get in, we ask to see him and we have a conversation. What could possibly go wrong? If he's as approachable as everyone thinks there shouldn't be a problem." Millewa spoke to all of them now.

"I think we send Millewa in." Everyone stopped chewing and stared at Sydare, this didn't bother him to continue on "It makes sense. Finfudune knew her dad and everything he believed in, she knows what to say, she's the most passionate elf I've ever seen on a subject and I think we'd be stupid to believe any of us could do a better job convincing him. In saying that, we need to have a backup plan if things go wrong. He may seem all sweet and caring, but I've heard far too many rumours of him being evil to not go in prepared"

"I'll do it." Millewa looked directly at Sydare. "What's the plan?"

As a team, they sat next to the fire for hours, working out contingencies and what to do if things went wrong. They decided to play on Millewa's innocence and send her to The King to schmooze his ego and win him over. In case of an emergency, Millewa would send an elf flare into the sky in hopes Alvie would reach them in time. It's all they had and they had to believe it would work.

Millewa's eyes grew tired and heavy and she could barely keep them open as the warmth of the fire encapsulated her. She got up, brushed her teeth and rolled into bed, the blankets clinging to every part of her, holding the warmth of the fire against her. She could hear Bee and Phlox's miniscule snores as she turned to the window and stared out it.

"Are you sure we're safe here?" Millewa yawned, she was minutes away from a deep slumber.

"Completely. Rowena sold you a fool proof tent. It has an invisibility charm connected to it, so once someone enters, the tent becomes completely invisible to everyone else except those inside or who were there to see it built. You could leave and come back with a friend and they wouldn't be able to see it. Really neat magic in fact." Sydare yawned in reply, "We have a big day tomorrow. We'll reach Clara for sure. Try and get some rest."

Millewa looked to the sky, her eyelids beginning to close. Just as the warmth and exhaustion took over, her eyes sprang back open, staring once again out the window.

She could've been dreaming already, but she could've sworn she saw four, large, green eyes staring right back at her.

Chapter Fourteen
Kobold

Millewa awoke to panic and chaos the next morning. Phlox, Bee and Sydare were running around the tent in absolute mayhem, screaming and shouting at one another in nonsensical panic.

Millewa jumped from her bed, quickly pulling on the day's clothes and stopped squarely in front of Sydare as he swiped his open palm at Bee, trying to catch her in his fist.

"- You, you did it! I know you did. It's always *your* kind," Sydare spat at Bee, the words cutting through her, pain etched into her sweet, golden face.

"I *swear* to you Sydare, it wasn't us!" Bee pleaded, her eyes wide with fear and sadness.

Millewa scanned the room, her deep, blue eyes taking in all that happened. She could now see why Sydare was so angry and she could also see why Bee was so upset.

The tent had been ransacked, every inch turned upside down. Food lay strewn across the floor, blankets heaved off beds, backpacks upturned and as she settled on her own bag, horror struck her face as she realised they'd been robbed. The map and flares to ensure their safety amongst the casualties.

Millewa fell to her knees, forearms pressed to the floor as she sobbed, uncontrollable, full body sobs. They weren't even twenty-four hours in and the sheer enormity of their job at hand, hit her right in the stomach. Millewa vomited across the floor, too overwhelmed to keep calm.

"I thought you said this was safe." Millewa directed her attention to Sydare, looking up to his yellow eyes, her face pale and sweaty.

"I thought it was, I – I'm sorry," Sydare helped Millewa to her knees, grabbing her some water from the kitchen.

"Before I fell asleep," Millewa took a sip from her water, remembering what she saw right before bed. The image ingrained into her mind. "I saw four large, green eyes staring through my window."

"Kobold." Sydare whispered. "They're a sprite aren't they? An evil sort." He now rounded on Phlox and Bee again, "So you tell me, how this creature, who is in the same description category as you, has defiled our magical protection and robbed us in the dead of night? How can you honestly look at me and tell me you weren't involved?"

"*Of course* it was us," Phlox retaliated as he began skulking around the room, arms clenched to his side, fingers long and loosened, with a devilish grin appearing across his face. "We always hang out with the Kobold and talk about ways to inconvenience elves, look how similar we are."

"Kobold are a horrible, nasty creature," Bee pushed Phlox to the side, hitting him with impressive force and telling him to stop fooling around, "They are large and scaled, HUGE eyes and faces pulled in to an ugly snout. Their hands are like talons and they're about the size of an elf. So you tell me Sydare, *who* is more like who, because I am certainly *nothing* like a Kobold." Bee huffed, exasperated with rage.

Sydare stopped and stared at her.

"Sorry Bee, you know, I don't deal with change or my anger very well. This whole situation was completely unexpected." Sydare hung his head low, clearly embarrassed by the whole ordeal.

"You don't say?" Bee rolled her eyes, giving Sydare a slight punch to the arm, which of course felt like nothing more than a press.

The mood was sombre after breakfast. They ate in utter silence, scraping shards of cereal off the floor to fuel their bodies. The Kobold had taken everything and what they hadn't taken, they'd destroyed completely.

Bee continued to explain that Kobold were extremely clever, as sprites are and can sniff out magic in their area. The map and flares held supreme magical properties that directed the Kobold right to them, hiding in the trees around their base, the Kobold were there when the tent was constructed, thus they were able to enter.

The map and flares were crucial to their plan and Millewa didn't know how they'd continue without them.

Although depleted and on edge, the group were fortunate enough to have camped in a fruitful area. Literally full of fruit.

The day before they had climbed the mountain side from the West, ensuring they stuck to the river, what they hadn't noticed off the North side of the mountain was a low lying field full to the brim of vegetables patches and fruit trees. Sydare had said it must've been an old sprite camp that lay forgotten. The soil so rich and pure that food continued to grow, even due to the lack of tending. Pineapple plants littered the grounds and tomato vines entwined themselves between every luscious tree, limbs sagging from the weight of fruit. Being quick and strategic, they picked only what they needed and ate along the way.

Millewa was trudging through a pumpkin patch when she noticed a peculiar track laden down with what looked like animal prints. She tracked it with her eyes, sloping down over another ridge the footprints did not cease.

Apple in hand, Millewa silently tiptoed towards the edge, a steep drop, but not too far down that she would hurt herself. Millewa looked around to check on the others, to make sure they weren't watching her and she dropped onto her bottom and slid down to the bottom bank. Her heart was pounding so loudly, she feared that whatever she was tracking might find her first.

She continued along, still able to hear the chatter of Phlox and Bee, keeping her breathing even, until what lay right in front of her. Carved into the opposing side of the gully was a wide, darkened cave entry, blood smeared across the top with ivy growing thickly around the entry. The stone was scratched and marked as if something sharpened its talons here. That's when she heard the deep, roaring snores erupting from inside, a foul, dead smell filling her nostrils. Her eyes watered at the stench as she edged ever closer to the cave, her heart thumping now in her ears, the sound of her friends gone and the only sounds were her feet crunching the leaves and the rumble of the sleeping Kobold.

Millewa kept to the side of the cave as she entered, keeping her breath low and shallow so as not to wake the creature within. She had no idea what they were capable of, or what would happen to her if they woke up.

She shuddered at the thought.

It was dark, pitch black and Millewa couldn't see a thing. She wondered whether she should abandon her mission right now, but she knew they needed that map and she'd now come too far. How long would it be before Sydare noticed her missing? The eagle pin in her pocket began to buzz.

Another step.

Cool water trickled at her neck, freezing her bones as she waited for her eyes to adjust.

Another step.

She could now make out the creatures in front of her, curled and piled on top of one another like a litter of puppies.

Another step.

There it was. In the grasp of the largest Kobold. The magical map that ensured they find a way home. The eagle pin was uncontrollable, her whole pocket vibrated, buzzing loudly and continuously. Millewa tried to reduce the noise, something, anything. This stupid pin, she thought, would be the death of her. Why did it only buzz when potential death arose?

Millewa inched closer, trying not to slip on the wet stone that cased the floor. She looked down, watching her steps when right in front of her lay a water gun shaped object. The flares! She grabbed them quickly and tucked them into her pack, making sure the safety feature was on and the flare didn't go off in the cave.

The Kobold's snoring continued, loud and monstrous, a shiver working its way down Millewa's spine, how was she to get the map without waking it? Then, she remembered what Sydare had said that morning when he ranted about Kobold's and their properties. *To disarm them, you simply pinch their ears together atop their head. Knocks them out cold.*

Millewa heard the voice clearly in her head, she needed to pinch the ears of the alpha and take the map. Easy. The pin buzzed as if agreeing with her thoughts.

Millewa held her breath. Her chest was tight with fear and she let out small gasps of air to curb her nausea. Her eyes had fully adjusted to the darkness now and she watched her feet to not step on the paws and talons that flailed everywhere.

There must've been ten Kobold piled up, this wasn't going to be easy, she thought. Millewa dropped to her hands and knees, crawling across the moss covered stones like a dog, her knees slightly giving way under the slippery floor. She was inches away from the head Kobold and a huge, heaving sigh erupted from its nostrils, coating her in thick, sticky goo that had shot out of its nose. Snot. Gross.

Millewa stabilised her left hand on the stone, her fingers twitching and aching from the cold, while her right hand, outstretched, pinched the ears together. The alpha's breathing stopped, the scent of death lingering from its final heave.

This was it.

This was Millewa's only chance to get the map back. She rose onto her shins, freeing her left hand to get the map. Millewa stopped breathing, cheeks puffed, she tentatively tugged at the map that rested between the long, spindly legs of the Kobold. Careful not to tear, she shimmied it out, folding it clumsily with one hand and stuffing it in her pocket. Sydare hadn't mentioned how to get out of this mess once you'd disarmed them. Millewa took her chances and released the Kobold's ears. A disgruntled snarl exploded from the Kobold, echoing and vibrating the cave walls surrounding them. The eagle pin didn't budge at all.

Millewa had to get out.

And fast.

She leapt to her feet, not worrying how much noise she made when the Kobold's large green eyes now narrowed on her position. Millewa scrambled, running for the cave light as quickly as she could, slipping and sliding across the slimy floor she heard the groan of the Kobold rising to its feet. Millewa didn't dare turn around. Didn't dare look into the eyes of the beast that had stalked them in the night.

Although they were no bigger than Millewa herself, their teeth were sharp like needles and threatened harm as they bared them at her.

A few more feet and she'd be at the entry of the cave once more. The light blinding her as she ran from extreme dark to light. The snarls and growls continued behind her and she knew she had to keep running, her lungs burning and legs aching. An echoed howl cascaded through the gully in which she ran, stinging her ears as it pierced her senses. She had to pick up the pace if they were indeed continuing to chase.

Breathless.

Her legs giving way, she kept running until she ran into something solid.

"There you are!" Sydare, she had barrelled body solid into Sydare.

"Quick – no time – Kobold – coming" Millewa said between exasperated, heaving breaths.

"Kobold? What are you on about?" Sydare looked over Millewa, making sure she wasn't hurt. Millewa pulled the crumpled map from her pocket, near throwing it at Sydare as she struggled to regain her breath. "You got the map back? How on earth?" Another loud, booming howl. "Never mind, let's get going!" Sydare took Millewa's arm and steered her back up the embankment.

Millewa dared one last glance toward the cave, the opening dark as it was before, except for two bulging green eyes and rows of dirty, white, needle pointed teeth.

Chapter Fifteen

Clara In Caligine

"What happened to you? We were whistling away enjoying the fruits of our labour – pun intended – and we turn around and you're gone!" Phlox was nearly beside himself when Sydare half dragged Millewa through the vegetable patch back to the mountain flat. He kept cursing himself for not paying attention and eating too many kiwi berries as they 'always sent him hyper' in his words.

"I found tracks in the pumpkins and, well, I don't know I was just drawn to follow them. Like I knew something was at the other end. I didn't know the map would be with them and I don't even know what I was expecting to find but I'm glad I went." Millewa replied.

"We're glad you went too. Not for the nearly having your head ripped off part, but I don't think any of you realised how utterly screwed we are without that map. My memory can only get us so far," Sydare smiled lazily at Millewa, she had once again proven her bravery and sheer stupidity was useful, even if she didn't have any powers.

"Let's make sure that if we are found by the Kobold, or any of The King's cronies again, this map won't be taken from us." Sydare held out the map to Bee, as if in silent agreement and understanding,

Bee took the map in her hands, twirled it on one finger and with a *pop* the map vanished. Bee opened her tiny pockets and dropped something, completely invisible inside.

"Awesome." Millewa chuckled.

The hike up the rest of the mountain was tiring, the steep incline was ten times as long as the one they'd endured yesterday.

The day was milder today, a cool breeze kissing their faces as their heavy leaden legs trudged up the mountain. The sky a pale, powder blue that stretched as far as they could see, the sun hidden behind a grey hue of cloud. The only sounds that surrounded them were the scrape of their boots across the hard, rocky surface and the wind that whistled atop the hills.

Millewa peeled off her jacket, stuffing it in her already full pack, despite the coolness of the day, she was sweating beneath her layers.

"Where is it you guys live exactly?" Millewa directed at Bee, "You always flew in my window so early."

Bee stifled a smile and tried not to laugh. "Have you not seen us around? We live in Dewdrop, just like you." Millewa felt instantly bad, she hadn't seen them around before and didn't want them thinking it was because of their size.

"I knew you must've been close and I'd obviously seen sprites throughout the day in the main square but… never where you lived." Millewa shrugged.

"Hehe, that's okay! We live in different parts of Dewdrop, we're all spread around actually. Water sprites are situated on the river edge, small mud houses built from sticks and clay. They're small but super cosy. Tree sprites, are, well slightly more wealthy and are situated in the trees limbs, we need far less space so we don't reside in the trunks like elves do." Bee struggled not to smile.

"*We* as in you," Phlox snorted, "Us water sprites are a simple people and are *much* poorer than tree sprites. Stuck up woodwork dwellers. It's a wonder Bee is even allowed to talk to me considering our social standings."

"Yes, yes we come from different backgrounds, you're annoying like a brother which means I'm still obliged to love you." Bee rolled her eyes and grinned at Phlox. "Anyways Millewa, have you not seen the pulley systems, magical fountains, healing stations and the fairy lights that litter the skies at night? That's all work of sprites keeping the place running. You elves would be living like heathens without us." Bee laughed, then did Phlox and finally Sydare let out a thunderous laugh that had us all in stitches.

"She's honestly not wrong," Sydare agreed, and for the first time ever, Millewa saw Sydare genuinely smile at the sprites with adoration in his eyes.

The four of them laughed and giggled until their voices were hoarse. Sharing stories about school life, their hands on learning and how different all their parents treated them. There was no talk of threats, of the wars gone by or anything that would elude to a dangerous situation. It was pure happiness and joy that had overcome them as they reached the peak of the mountain.

Exhausted, covered in sweat and needing a drink, they stopped just before the top, marvelling at the progress they had made that day, despite the grim start.

"Just over this peak, we'll be able to see Clara" Sydare choked out as he took another huge gulp of water. "You'll want to remember the first time you experience it, it's a sight to behold. It stands in its own valley, surrounded by farms and trees. Luscious, green, sweeping plains, an oasis in the middle of the barren lands we've crossed. Don't be fooled by its beauty though, The King no doubt has protection around the edges, his perfect land, he will want it to remain untouched from prying eyes and feet." Sydare warned.

They packed away their bottles, securing them tightly with an outside strap of their pack. Millewa slung it over her back and took a deep breath. A few more steps and she would be at the peak of the mountain, soon to be looking over the plateau that is Clara. Soon enough, she would be knocking on the doors of The Wizard Kingdom pleading for freedom. She looked to her friends and smiled, they were ready too.

The scene was breathtaking.

Open, rolling fields of green flooded the valley below, trees bordered the area and lined each twisting cobblestone road that lead towards the city itself. Small cottages were placed sporadically in the fields, brown wooden fences bordering the lands edge. The sweet scent of dew and honey wafting to their noses and dizzying their thoughts. Amid the rolling fields, tree mazes and fruit paddocks was where it stood. Clara.

Millewa couldn't believe her eyes or behold to the beauty that lay at the other end of the plateau. A castle as white as snow towered above all the rest, protected by a thick pearl coloured wall that encircled the entire city. Millewa could just make out the houses and townhouses that lined the grey shaded streets and flowers of crystal and amber were visible from where they stood. Her heart skipped a beat and she was excited and enticed to press on, to see within the city walls, to smell the flowers and eat their food. She couldn't wait much longer and took a step toward the city, her mouth dry with anticipation. They would make it there today and she could live as the rich did.

A thin haze broke over the mountain top, rain, Millewa thought must be coming, they were so high up it would hit them first.

Millewa turned to Phlox, Bee and Sydare who were all behind her, cheeks puffed and eyes wild. They were amazed as she was. Except they weren't, their eyes weren't wide in amazement, Millewa realised. Their eyes were wide with panic.

"Millewa, hold your breath, Millewa" Sydare's voice was

slow and drawn out as if someone had put him in slow motion. "Millewa."

Her vision began to blur, her friends in front of her looked like blobs of colour against the beautiful sky. Everything around her was distorted, her head feeling heavy as if someone had placed a brick where her brain was. Her eyes glazed, trying to blink away water but she couldn't, she was fading and she could feel it. Millewa put her hands out in front of her, where her fingers should be she could only see a blur of beige and she looked to Sydare, hoping he'd have an answer for it all.

"Help me," Millewa's voice was like tar against her mouth, the words escaping at a glacial pace. Panic overcame her senses, twisting and turning she looked to anything for help. Bile began to rise from her stomach and she thought she may be sick. Twice in one day. Great. Someone stood in front of her, grasping her shoulders so tight she may scream.

Sydare.

"Millewa, can you hear me? Are you okay? Millewa!" She knew he was shouting, yelling at her and gripping her to try and help her escape this mania, but all she could hear were drawn out screams that she realised were coming from her own mouth. Her voice was nearly raw from shrieking. "Millewa focus, focus on me, please."

Panic. This time from Sydare.

Millewa started to close her eyes, the weight of all too much for her to take anymore, she wanted to sleep, she felt so tired, so heavy, so groggy. A small, winged creature of purple and green flew in between her and Sydare, its wings beating, thunderous in her ears. She tried to focus on this tiny thing, to see what it was doing. Phlox cupped his hands before his face, and gave a great, shuddering breath. Glittering, purple dust bellowed from his hands, coating Millewa's face.

Sleep. Her mind told her, before she toppled to the ground.

Chapter Sixteen

The City of Magic

An icy blast splashed Millewa in the face, she had barely caught her breath from the shock when her head was quickly and violently plunged into a frost bitten stream that awakened all her senses immediately. Gasping for air and struggling to open her eyes, Millewa was dunked again. This time fully aware of what was happening to her, she jerked back, kicking behind her at whatever held her hair in a fist. She connected with something hard and flipped over as she heard them thud to the ground.

"*Ow.*" Sydare groaned from the ground, holding his knee in protest. Millewa sat bolt upright, looking to her friend.

"I'm sorry Sydare!" Millewa crawled to his side "I thought someone was trying to drown me."

"Cold water immersion," Sydare winced "That's the only way to wake someone up from In Caligine, The Fog."

"The what?" Millewa pressed.

"In Caligine is one of The King's more well-known protective charms, I was so excited to show you the view I'd forgotten he'd likely have that circling." Sydare now sat up, looking to Millewa. "It's a charm that covers all of Clara's edges - except for the main road in - ensuring any unwanted visitors are knocked out and dragged before The King. It's a harmful delusion that sends the receiver mad. I was far enough back when it creeped over the edge, I was able to hold my breath and take you to safety. Phlox hit you with a stunning dust to make you pass out, calming your racing heart and stopping your breath intake, it's what saved you."

"Plus, sprites don't get knocked over by those charms so we had time to think." Phlox added.

"You don't?" Sydare rounded on Phlox "Never mind that now."

"Finfudune Bosmerch does not consider sprites as equal or better and does not consider warding us off against these protective charms. That's how much he's sees us as a threat." Phlox's cheeks were suddenly flushed with colour, "The nerve of him honestly. Sprites create these charms; he makes us do his dirty work. Good for us though that the captive sprites in Clara leave it open for us, and that I'm a genius and know the counter spell."

Millewa's face burned red with embarrassment. She was the only one out of them all to not realise the fog was creeping towards them, she was too distracted by the castle walls to see that she was being poisoned. Sydare could see her flushed face and put his arm around her shoulders, silently reassuring her it's okay.

The water was fresh and brisk as Millewa dipped her toes in. She hadn't bathed in a couple of days now and felt dirty. If they were certainly meeting The King later that day, she needed to be presentable and not covered in sweat and dirt. Along with Bee, she headed towards an isolated part of the stream where they could bathe in peace away from the boys.

Bee used her powers to conjure some washing dust and within minutes, Millewa was fully submerged. Her teeth chattering and cold to the bone, she used the dust to wash herself and her hair, pulling chunks of mud as she did.

"This is gross" Millewa said to Bee as she dragged a large, slimy piece of mud from her scalp. "How am I so dirty?!"

"You did fall remember, into a big old dirt patch too" Bee giggled. Millewa liked having Sydare as her friend, but boy was it good to have a friend that was also a girl. She could see herself and Bee becoming really good friends.

Shivering, the girls got out of the stream, Bee summoning fresh clothes that she'd pre heated. They got dressed and evaluated one another before heading back to the main section. Millewa looked down at herself, impressed with the finery she now adorned for her arrival to the city. Brown leather sandals covered her feet, cream coloured, long ribbed pants and a flowing linen shirt tucked in at the sides. Her hair was neatly braided at the top, with gold pins holding the folds in place. Her eyes sparkled against the sun's rays.

“Well, well,” Sydare said to Millewa as he looked her up and down “Someone is ready to meet The King. Shall we?” Sydare held out his arm, Millewa grabbed a hold and they headed to the main road in. No fog or mist would get them this time.

The edge of Clara showed a stark contrast between where they’d come from to where they were going. A brown field behind them, a green oasis in front. Millewa spotted a large rock at the edge and decided they should leave their bags behind it and grab them on their way out. There was no point wearing fine clothes and jewellery, whilst looking shabby with a backpack. They didn’t plan on staying overnight so they wouldn’t need their supplies. Sydare pocketed some money in case they wanted food and stuffed the bags between the rock and hill.

They walked through fields of blueberries, strawberries, blackberries and kiwi berries on their way to the front gates. Phlox and Bee sat on Millewa’s shoulders with their eyes closed, not wanting to take in the brutality that faced their kind. Sprites worked tirelessly in the fields, chained together by glowing steel that wouldn’t let them stray more than a metre. Some with their wings clipped, those who had defied The King or dared try to escape. Hunched over, exhausted and dirty, they picked berries and placed them in woven baskets, ready to be sent to The King. Slaves. Millewa realised. This was Phlox and Bee’s reason for being here.

“Tell me when we’re past it all.” Bee whimpered. The crunch of golden gravel beneath their sandals the only sound they could hear. Millewa smiled at each sprite that dared look up, sadness shrouded their faces, their skin dark and leathery from working under the beating sun. It looked like they had never eaten, their sunken bodies wrinkled and aged with lack of food.

Millewa quickened her step.

She wanted to be out of there as soon as possible.

Millewa took a long, deep inhale when they reached the gates to the city. Towering over them stood a golden barred gate that glowed and pulsated with magic and protective charms. It must have cost an absolute fortune to make, Millewa thought. To the left of the gate stood a white stone pillar with clear glazed windows that harboured the same magical effect as the gate. This was it. The moment of truth and what Millewa had feared from the moment they'd agreed to confront The King. Millewa approached the windowed pillar, she could make out a fat wizard sitting behind the glass, biscuit and tea in his hands, crumbs sprinkled all through his wiry-brown moustache. She gave a sharp rap on the glass, stepping back quickly to get a full view of the wizard inside.

"Name?" The pompous wizard questioned as he slid the glass back, just enough so Millewa could make out his charcoal coloured eyes.

"Millewa Cornell sir. I'm here to see King Finfudune" Millewa plastered her sweetest smile on her face, trying not to wince as the wizard slurped his tea, droplets soaking onto his chin.

"An elf, hey? Your kind aren't welcome here without invitation from The King himself. See to it that you vacate these lands *immediately*." The round faced wizard shut the glass window sharply and with purpose. Millewa turned around to Sydare, face sunken and defeated.

"Try again, you have to insist!" Sydare whispered back to her. Millewa turned on her heel, striding towards the glass once more with fierce determination.

Tap. Tap. Tap.

Millewa clicked the glass in rapid succession.

"Name? Oh no not you again," the wizard made to close the glass before Millewa had the chance to speak. Filled with rage and embarrassment, Millewa forced her hand between the glass panel and the stone wall in which it clicked into. Pushing back with all her mite.

"Excuse me sir, I'm fearful you didn't hear me. I am here to see The King." Millewa kept her stance firm. The wizard behind the glass began to smile, in fact, he began laughing uncontrollably. The only words he uttered were choked by sweeps of laughter as he imitated Millewa in a high pitched baby voice.

"Why would our lord, King Finfudune want to speak to four children? No less *elves* and *sprites*. Ridiculous." The grumpy wizard grumbled.

SLAM.

The glass rattled in Millewa's face, near shattering from the force in which he closed it. Millewa huffed a huge sigh and straightened her back and held her shoulders back. She would not be forgotten or pushed aside.

Not anymore.

Tap. Tap. Tap.

The same wizard guard appeared in the glass frame again.

"Now young lady I have told you already-" he started.

"No, it's time you stopped grumbling and listen!" Millewa shouted in his face. "I travelled all this way from Dewdrop Springs to see The King. I know he is a graceful, kind and compassionate man who is always there for his people. He would not turn his back on me or my friends, he would welcome our visit with great value. I have an issue I need help with, so, if you please, open the darned gate." Millewa turned to face the wizard again, her face hot and flushed. If he didn't let her in after that rant, there was no hope and they may as well pack up and go home.

Except, the wizard guard no longer stood there, instead, in his place was none other than King Finfudune himself.

"How correct you are young Millewa" Finfudune's sparkling white teeth bared down on Millewa and blinded her from the window in which he stood. "It is so good to see you once again, this time in a much prettier and upbeat land, Clara. Please, please come through."

Millewa fashioned a sweet smile at The King, realising his compliment was back handed and eluding to Dewdrop Springs as a dump site. Nonetheless, he was going to let them through. The golden gates rattled with immense pressure, the solid latch clicking open. They squeaked and groaned as they heaved open, scraping slightly along the cobblestone path. A shimmery, glittered veil fell from the top of the gate, pooling on the ground at their feet, they knew now the protective charm had fallen and they were clear to enter the city. One by one they crossed over the threshold, stepping warily over the pearly-white mass that laid at their toes.

The city was even more beautiful than Millewa had imagined when she stood atop the mountains earlier that day.

A huge monument fountain was the centrepiece of the entrance, an ode to King Finfudune and his consort. The cobblestone paths laden with tulips of every colour and the surrounding buildings made of a stark white stone. Ivy tickled the edges of the outer wall and twisted with passionfruit vines amongst the wizarding homes. The scent of citrus filled the air and Millewa noticed lemon trees dotted amongst the grassy nature strips that lined the streets edge. Stone wizard monuments were built tall at each street corner, bronze plaques screwed to their bases. Memorials for the fallen wizards of the war, a tribute to those who died fighting.

Millewa wondered if her father would be credited by a statue for his heroism. From sight of all the wizards and lack of other creatures, she thought not. Bluebirds chirped overhead and Millewa couldn't believe the sanctuary and feeling of security.

Wizards passed, nodding and bowing to The King on their way. Women dressed in long, flowing gowns with their loosely curled hair clipped back by a single claw of an unknown creature. Men were adorned in lightly coloured slacks and tight fitting shirts, accompanied by a bow tie or free flowing collar.

They were beautiful and powerful, every single one of them. Their life here was perfect and they wandered about without a care in the world. She must have been gaping for a while, not even noticing The King's pale green eyes staring straight at her. Millewa gave a slight jump when she caught his gaze.

"Incredible isn't it?" Finfudune beamed at his city, the one he'd snatched right beneath King Wozil's burning body.

"It is lovely, sir. Truly." Millewa wasn't lying, the pureness and serenity that the city encapsulated did make Dewdrop Springs seem lesser.

"Might I show you around? We can chat about your urgent matters along the way?" Finfudune offered his arm to Millewa, which she took with gratitude as he steered her to the left of his statue. She couldn't be quite sure, but she could've sworn she saw the darn thing wink.

The King walked slowly around the streets of Clara, pointing out all of his most favourite spots to Millewa. He spoke to her as if Sydare, Phlox and Bee weren't trailing a metre behind them.

First, they toured the bakery end, where sprites were busied with baking bread and tarts, selling their wares at an insanely cheap price. Butternut croissants, candied apple bread and toasted sesame lava cakes laden the front window, wafts of fresh bread and nutmeg consuming Millewa's senses. Millewa thought she heard Phlox mumble about how sprite food used to be an Autumn Market specialty, not an everyday endeavour. They swept along the West Side Village where wizard children were playing with wands, battling one another with spark shooting. Millewa smiled, remembering how her siblings used to pretend old knife sharpeners were wands and they'd fly about the house throwing fake spells at one another.

She gave a great sigh at the thought of her human family, probably smiling and laughing more than they ever had now that she wasn't there to burden them. It all seemed too fantastical, too incredible that she was here and she felt the most overwhelming sense of happy and calm.

"I'm surprised you made it here safely," The King turned his attention to Millewa, stopping out the front of an ice cream shop and pulling out a white, iron stool for her. The patterns on the back of the chair twisted intricately to depict The King's quarters.

"Mmm?" Millewa perused the menu, licking her lips at the delectable flavours. Honey blueberry peanut butter crunch sounded like a winner to her. She was so engaged in her taste buds she didn't even realise Sydare, Phlox and Bee must have trailed elsewhere from being continually ignored.

"Yes, very surprised. You know, my lands are abundant and great but the threat of the orcs is still ever so present." Finfudune pressed on as Millewa's large ice cream was plopped in front of her by a silver haired sprite in black cloth. Nothing like the beautiful garments the sprites wore in Dewdrop, shabby, Millewa thought. She grabbed a silver spoon and began taking great mouthfuls of her creamy treat. "Orcs are nasty creatures, with blood on their minds. You have done remarkably well to get here unharmed."

"It was quite a journey, but we managed." Millewa said between mouthfuls of ice cream, The King looked down his nose in disgust. This is why he hated children, so easily entertained by sugar and sweets. "I mean, we had our run ins don't get me wrong. Amarok, Kobold and not to mention that nasty fog that nearly sent me loopy on the top of the mountain."

"Ah? In Caligine got you did it?" Finfudune grinned as Millewa nodded, "Sorry about that. You know my people must be protected and outsiders are no exception. Next time you wish to visit, please just send a raven to request. Or I think you elves prefer the use of doves."

"That's incredibly kind, sir" Millewa wiped her mouth as the final dribbles of dessert slipped down her chin. She was full and content having not eaten a decent meal since leaving Dewdrop.

"Shall I show you the castle now? The final stop of the tour. Then we can meet tomorrow in regards to your questions," The King stood and once again offered his lanky arm to Millewa, robes hanging loose from his skin.

"Tomorrow? We weren't planning on staying overnight your highness." Millewa looked around for a sign of Sydare.

“Oh nonsense, you won’t make it far tonight at any matter. See the sky beginning to wane and the sun dipping? It’ll be dark in no time. In fact, your friends are already at the doors waiting to be seen to their quarters.” Good, Millewa thought. Relieved at the fact she wasn’t separated from her friends. She walked through the darkening streets to the grand stone steps leading to the huge oak doors that split The King from everyone else.

“After you,” The King ushered. The heavy doors crashed shut with a solid thud. Everything inside was dark.

Chapter Seventeen
The Eagle is Watching

The entry sprang to life, light filling the corners and beholding the beauty and elegance of the castle. A large room filled with oil candles marked the beginning of the journey into the castle. Hallways and doors led off the circle room in directions to the left and right and before them stood a sweeping staircase of marble and stone, guiding them to what Millewa could only assume as the living sector.

If Millewa thought the city of Clara was luxurious, it was nothing compared to where she had stepped into.

Dark floors laden with thick, rich carpets. Oil paintings of kings gone by, adding colour and life to the papered walls. Gold and silver danced along the walls, eluding to the exquisite wealth and Millewa nearly fell over at the size of the diamond crusted chandelier that hung high in the air.

Sydare, Phlox and Bee entered the open expanse from the left, grinning sheepishly at Millewa as they were reunited. She had wondered how long they had been in the castle before her arrival.

"Shall we?" The King's voice sliced the air and Millewa gave a little jump. Blushing from her embarrassment she nodded to The King and allowed him to lead the way. "My castle is small, as you may see, compared to most other ruling kings. It was rebuilt after that dreadful Autumn day and I was specific in saying 'I need not more than any ordinary man,' of course, I *am* no ordinary man. Nonetheless, a smaller residence it was. I have twelve guest rooms, all overlooking the city and all decorated to match the visitor's lands. You can imagine the sprite visiting quarters are *filthy*." Finfudune gave a great chuckle.

Phlox and Bee scowled in his direction.

"Yes, well." He continued on, "the living section is up those stairs and to the left. My living quarters harbour the whole right side of the upper building. To our left" Finfudune began to lead the way where her friends had just come from, "you'll find the kitchens and dining room, able to seat fifty guests at once."

Millewa popped her head in and was overwhelmed with the size of the room, it was huge and decorated in a similar fashion to the front entry.

"These double doors to the right," The King pressed on, now leading them back into the foyer, "they lead to our ballroom. I'm not shy about throwing grand parties and my Spring Ball is quite a hit, although it has been a few years since that has happened."

His brow furrowed slightly, before he snapped out of it and began grinning once more.

"My office is straight up the stairs and directly in front. Only I can enter with a specific spell, protective charms are cast all through the city and particularly this building. You'd surely understand that after the war." He smiled at them all and clasped his hands, "Well, my slave – I mean servant, Lantana will show you to your rooms."

A small sprite, no older than eighteen stood before them. Her golden hair draped at her sides, her moth eaten clothes of black looked like she had never worn anything else.

"Please follow me." And so they did.

They were all placed in separate rooms. Millewa was in the furthest down the hall and to the left with Bee's room next door and Sydare and Phlox across from them.

Her room mirrored that of which was in Alvie and Berrima's home. Chocolate wooden floors that were rough and bumped with grooves of wood grain, whispering stories of their past to her.

Voluptuous cream curtains swung slightly in the breeze from the open window that looked over the park below. A four poster bed stood tall in the room, its bed sheets of ivory and blush crinkled against one another in dreamy folds.

The walls were a forest green, golden paint cascaded across the surface in thin lines, creating a mural of an eagle watching over her every move.

She felt as though she was being watched, its eyes unmoving yet its presence was lively. She pulled the pin from deep in her pockets and flipped it over in her hand. What on earth could it mean?

Millewa thought of the danger she may be in and the pin jumped slightly in her hand as if to say it agreed.

Millewa wandered her room, taking in every tiny detail until her stomach grumbled in protest. She'd only had some fruit and ice cream and yearned for something more substantial.

She grabbed her stomach as another loud grumble erupted and in response a wooden tray appeared on her bed, the same colour as the floors. Within seconds the tray was full of food and sweets, tempting her to dive right in.

Piping hot stew, warm, fresh bread, tea biscuits and scones filled her belly as it sang to her in pleasure. She had never eaten such wonderful and flavourful food, she had wondered if her new favourite was this, rather than Stella's spaghetti Bolognese. Her heart twinged with pain at the thought of her adoptive mother and she pushed the thought right from her mind.

She had a new home now, a better one.

When her plates were clear and her belly full, the tray disappeared, only to reappear moments later with a painted porcelain teapot, cup and saucer. Decorated with what she recognised to be Alvie's vegetable patch in Dewdrop Springs, she wondered if Sydare was receiving the same treatment.

She poured herself a cup, soaking in the scent of lavender and myrtle, she carried her tray towards the bathroom that led off from her room. Placing it steadily on the stool beside the bath, Millewa turned the handles of the taps and let the water run freely and steaming into the large claw footed bathtub below.

Salts, soaps and shampoos appeared in mid-air, teasing Millewa to put them in the water. She chose a wood smoked apple salt that turned the water fuchsia and a prickly pear shampoo that soothed her hair delicately.

Sinking lower in the bath, bubbles rising all around her, Millewa grabbed her cup of tea. She drank deeply from her cup and closed her eyes, paying attention to the aromas that filled the air, relaxing every inch of her body.

Before she knew it, a wave of exhaustion crashed over her and she fell into a dizzying dream of Kobolds and fog and the cup of tea smashed onto the bone coloured floor.

Chapter Eighteen

Wind and Fire

Birds chirping filled the air and Millewa awoke groggy and bleary eyed. She looked to the window to see a raven perched on the ledge, a note bound to its leg with bright red ribbon.

Millewa rolled from the comfort and cosiness, rubbing her eyes and yawning. She had fallen asleep in the bathtub last night, yet she woke around midnight tucked into bed like a child. How she got there she would never know, but it gave her an uneasy feeling deep in the pit of her stomach.

The raven was the colour of ebony, its feather sleek and shiny, reflecting the harsh light of the morning sun.

Millewa kept an eye on the bird's beak whilst she attempted to free the note that was latched to its leg. After a minor struggle, the parchment was free and Millewa unfurled it and read:

Meet me in my office not long after you wake. Lantana has already laid out your clothes by the dresser.

Your King,

Finfudune.

Millewa stared at the note, then to the dresser, where sure enough an outfit of linen and pearl was straightened and waiting for her.

She gulped the orange juice and munched the toast that appeared on her bed moments later and hurriedly brushed her teeth before getting dressed. It wasn't Millewa's first choice for an outfit but it was comfortable all the same.

A shin length skirt of silky fabric that glittered like pearls of the sea, accompanied by a simple white singlet that tucked nicely beneath the waistband.

Sandals waited by the door in a silvery glow and they looked as if they had been carved of marble, yet they were soft as clouds. Millewa grabbed a pearl crusted head band from the dresser drawer and pushed her short hair from her face.

She felt as though she could live in Clara if this was the treatment she'd receive.

A princess. She felt like a princess.

Sydare was already waiting in the hall when Millewa emerged from her room. He looked her up and down and shrugged. She assumed that meant her outfit was acceptable.

Sydare had been given the same expectations it seems, light brown slacks and a white shirt, his long brown locks tied into a low, loose bun. His yellow eyes twinkled in the candle light as they made their way down the hall.

"I didn't see you much at all yesterday. Not really, anyways." Sydare grumbled, "Anyone would think The King wants you all to himself!"

"It was a bit odd wasn't it, anywho, he clearly invited you to this meeting this morning. Why else would you be ready at the same time?" Millewa joked, Sydare was so funny with her sometimes, like an overprotective big brother.

"What meeting? I had no invitation of the sort. I've been standing outside your room for fifteen minutes waiting for you to hurry up so we can get out of here." Sydare narrowed his eyes on her, he didn't trust what had been happening in Clara and wanted to leave as soon as possible.

"I didn't get a chance to raise my case with King Bosmerch last night, he was more interested in our trip here than coming to understand what I was requesting." Millewa said "He sent me a note this morning to see him in his office as soon as I was ready."

"I certainly didn't receive that memo." Sydare slumped.

The pair walked the hall in silence, taking in the images of past visitors, Millewa's parents amongst those painted.

She stared at them for a while, they looked happy, content and strong it seemed. She smiled at their image, taking a mental note of their features, she looked just like her mum.

Chattering wings filled the hall with noise. The silence broken by two spritely creatures who tumbled out of their bedrooms to join them. Their clothes, of course, were exactly the same as yesterday.

"Fool tried to get us to wear black," Phlox spat. "Is he kidding? No way I'm sporting that slave uniform."

Bee seemed to have the same idea. Finfudune really did see sprites as lesser beings.

"I'm ready to get out of here in fact," Bee added "I've had enough of this backwards city to last a life time."

"Millewa's meeting is this morning, I say we all join and then the minute it's over, we get out of here!" Sydare looked to them all.

"Deal." Phlox and Bee replied in unison.

The four reached the end of the hall, meeting the grand marble staircase to the foyer below. A sharp left turn saw them standing right before Finfudune's office where he'd asked to meet.

The door bore no handles or door knobs and Millewa wondered how on earth anyone got into the room at all.

Her thoughts were cut short when they flung open with impressive force, only to see another, smaller sitting room with another door to enter through to the main part of the office. Standing before them was The King himself, head to toe in fiery red, the same that held Millewa's note together.

"Ah Millewa, I trust you got my note. Lantana has once again done wonderfully in dressing our guests." He looked to both Sydare and Millewa in adoration. "I shan't keep you any longer than necessary, please come through."

The four of them made a start forward when The King turned back to face them.

"Not you three, just Millewa," he added kindly.

"We all believe we should be there" Sydare retorted bravely.

"I understand, but Millewa is the one who was brave enough to seek me out and to stand up to the guards yesterday. She has an idea and questions, so she alone will meet with me. Feel free to peruse the foyer, goodbye." With that, Finfudune closed the first double doors in Sydare, Phlox and Bee's face and leaves them to twiddle their thumbs outside the office chamber.

Millewa stood in Finfudune's office, it was enormous and filled with light.

Bookshelves rose to the ceiling; like those she had seen in her parent's memorial library. Every piece of furniture was made of wood or ivory or marble and tapestries of the finest materials hung by the doors.

Millewa looked to the broad window that covered the wall behind The King's desk. A glass window with countless panes brought together by wooden accents. It was a sight to behold.

What Millewa was truly drawn to was the centre of the glass, where a strange oblong shape of stained glass sat starkly against the clarity of the clear glass.

The King could see Millewa staring at it, her face mesmerised and confused.

"Ah yes, it is unfortunate. We wanted to make a proper memorial for our dear deceased King Wozil, this is the site where he was pushed from the window by the orcs and savagely killed. This stained glass mural serves as a reminder that this can happen and it is so important to keep order and security over the kingdom." King Bosmerch bowed his head in grave dismay.

"That's exactly what I wish to talk to you about, King Bosmerch." Millewa shuddered.

The King gestured for Millewa to sit, so she pulled at the heavy chair that sat opposite Finfudune, looking across the desk. "You see, sir I don't feel that justice or freedom was brought to the sprites and elves through this whole ordeal."

"Oh?" Finfudune managed to say.

"Yes, in fact I believe it would be better if they lived freely and without contempt amongst the lands as it once was and as my father wished it. Sir." Millewa's whole body was shaking, she gripped her hands together to hide the ferocity in which they shook.

"Freedom? You think freedom is the answer?" Finfudune stood from his seat and look darkly at Millewa, the sparkle in his eyes dulling by the second. His white teeth turning an awful shade of grey.

"I truly do." Millewa held his gaze, not backing down from what she believed to be right.

"How dare you," The King spat the words like a snake spitting venom, "How dare you enter my lands, the lands I've sought to protect since your foolish father died, and demand freedom amongst the creatures I keep safe. How dare you believe you have any idea what is best for Apricus and all its beings."

Millewa was taken aback, realising the enormity of her request. Something inside her didn't want her to back down though. It may have been the eagle pin which she fashioned on her shoulder straps, or the fire her father passed down to her, but she was not in a position to be told no.

"I've heard what the people of Dewdrop Springs have had to say, they are unhappy, they are worked to their ends and they wish to be free of your reign. Sir." Millewa stood up, not nearly matching The King's height. She wanted to prove to him she wasn't backing down. "I wanted to talk to you about it first before you had a real revolt on your hands."

"And who died and made you Queen of Dewdrop then? Who gave you the right to speak to my people about such matters? What you're doing is treason and you'd best be minding your own business. You are but a child. Telling me how to run my lands, humph" The King scoffed. "Get out and go home girl. I've seen and heard enough."

"I'm not leaving until you free my people." Millewa stood her ground

"Your people? *YOUR PEOPLE*?" The King's face turned as scarlet as his robes, his neck bulging and eyes an inky black.

He was livid with rage and now pressed his hands firmly into the desk, staring at Millewa with pure hatred. "I knew you were trouble the minute Sydare found you in that forest. Your father was the same. Always dismissing what I had to say and scoffing at my opinions. Look who's alive and laughing now. It's my time and I won't have you stand in my way."

If Millewa had questioned his changing face before, she was sure of it now. Finfudune's once whitened teeth were a dark shade of grey. His bright, pale green eyes were as black as the night sky and his grey hair standing on end around his face.

He looked manic and powerful and Millewa felt a pit the size of a bowling ball tearing in her stomach.

The King was tall, more than doubling the height of Millewa and her elven frame. His hands began motioning, large, controlled strokes of the air that sent a blasting wind around the room.

Papers were torn from books, stationery fell from the desk and Millewa could see flames and fire burning behind Finfudune's ink black eyes.

She had seen once before an action like this and she knew he was about to cast a spell, about to blast her from the face of the earth and murder her in the dew of the morning.

Millewa put her arms up around her face, trying to protect herself at any cost. Eyes closed, wincing. Hands outstretched, as if pleading with The King to stop.

She felt hot, a burning sensation rippling through her body. It hurt so much she thought he may have set her on fire. Millewa opened her eyes to assess the damage to her body that was taking place. There they were.

Flames.

Except the flames weren't protruding from Finfudune at all. Roaring, crackling, white hot flames were emanating from Millewa's hands. Huge waves of heat in tightly spun tunnels were striking King Bosmerch right in the chest.

Millewa marvelled at what was happening. Phlox had been

correct, her fiery personality and stubbornness agreed. Her element was fire.

Finfudune fell backwards, a charred hole gaping in the centre of his blood red robes. His eyes were now wild with fury, his teeth gritted and low snarl roared from beneath the surface of his skin.

Millewa looked from The King to her hands. Charcoal coated her fingers with embers sizzling at the tips.

Shock and adrenaline began to take over and she looked from her hands just in time to see The King raising his hands in menacing rage.

A strong pushing motion forward and lightning exploded from King Bosmerch's hands, barrelling towards Millewa in an electrifying retaliation. Gold and yellow light spitting off in every direction, crackling and burning any surface it made contact with.

Millewa jumped for cover, ducking under the sideboard that lingered by the door to the room. Cowering in place, she had made it just in time, before Finfudune sent another deathly blow her way.

A field of glitter and glow surrounded Millewa and the sideboard, protecting them from the onslaught of magic that attempted to maim her, she had no idea where this force field came from but she imagined it were another extension of her powers.

She was so close to the door, now was her chance to escape. Millewa sprang from beneath the sideboard, hoping the force field around her would hold long enough to make it through the doors.

Gasping for air, she faced the large oaken doors and realised. There were no handles. She had seen this when she walked in but forgotten.

Was this his plan with any visitor to his office? To keep them locked in and to kill them if things didn't go his way?

Millewa slammed her fists against the door, furious at her stupidity and naivety.

The King was relentless, firing different spells continually at her shield. Varying colours and beams ricocheted off the surface and were destroying the room in which they stood. Bookshelves were burning, furniture was splintered and Millewa was positioned in the middle, once white clothing singed and torn, tears starting to burn behind her eyes. But there was no time for crying, no time to give in, today was not her day to die.

The King continued peppering her with enchantments, calculating her every move and following her ruthlessly around the expansive room.

Millewa ducked and weaved, hoping her shield would hold out long enough for her to formulate a plan. Her brain was working so fast on surviving, she barely had the chance.

She jumped behind a smaller desk on the right of the room, attempting to catch her breath before the next move. She looked to her hands, willing them to cast fire once more, but alas they stayed charcoal and wouldn't spark a flame.

The desk above her rose into the air, flying across the room and smashing into the bookcase adjacent. Millewa rolled from where she was and sprinted quickly to the other side of the room, pulling heavy, leather bound books from the shelf and heaving them at The King, trying to knock his concentration, trying to stop his imminent spells.

The King rounded on her, colour bubbling at his palms, rage and anguish painting his face.

She was going to die, there was no solution, there was no way. Millewa didn't know what to do, there was only one thing that sprang to her mind and so she did it.

She screamed.

A high pitched, screeching sound that pierced their ear drums and made them both stop dead. Finfudune's power dwindling to nothing as his hands fell lifelessly to his sides.

"Why are you doing this to me?" Millewa panted, she was exhausted, her energy drained and power limp against his. King Bosmerch's gaze met hers.

"I spent much of my life as The King's advisor back in a time when your parents lived." He took a deep inhale, as if calculating what he wanted to say. "That fool Wozil was a pain and often denied my wishes and advisories against his better judgement.

"That oaf never wanted any enslavement across the lands, he believed everyone to be equal. What nonsense he spun to the lands about being *friends* with one another. Well I knew better, I always knew better. Wizards are the top of the food chain, the supreme magical being, never to be messed with or to take orders.

"Wozil was so wrong, about so many things, particularly this. You are all imbeciles. Idiots. Sprites, elves and orcs and everything in between. You are lesser in this world and powerless to the magic in which we possess, that is why we have held you all for so long. "Look at you today, you cannot match me, you cannot beat me. You spent half your time running and crying rather than face me and why? You know your power will not stand up against the most powerful being in this land. You are defenceless, in my office, with no way out.

"Now I'm not going to throw that all away am I? Not because some born again elf thinks it's her birth right to take back the kingdom and make it equal again, especially because she thinks it'll please her dead dad." Millewa stood speechless, mouth open wide and in shock of what The King was saying to her.

She whimpered and shivered, what had she done? All for what?

"There is a reason this city burned those fifteen years ago and that was to make a point, to mark my reign. A new era has begun and *it is mine.*" Finfudune stood tall, taller than before and he filled the room, choking Millewa and her thoughts. She was overcome with claustrophobia and gasped for air.

"You… You did it. You set the city alight," she rasped. "It was you who let Clara burn. It was you who killed The King, not the orcs. You, who hated my father and his defiance, you killed him too." Millewa couldn't breathe.

Finfudune grinned his ugly, pale grey grin back at her, his eyes scarily wide and proud.

"How smart of you to figure it out. I knew you had it in you," he teased. "We could have been a powerful team had you not tried to ruin it with your insane ideology. It really is a shame you won't live long enough to tell anyone else you'd figured it out."

A bombardment of assault spells rained down from the ceiling, vibrant rays of pink, purple and red showered Millewa from above. Her protective shield was beginning to falter, thin, cracked lines appearing over the surface. She needed to get out. Fast.

The King's laughter shattered the room and another shower of spells spilt over the floor, grey light amongst the deadliest of spells. Millewa ducked for cover under his desk.

She had one move.

One idea.

The window.

Millewa scrambled from the ground, adjusting her skirt to free her legs. She charged at Finfudune, knocking him to the side as she made her exit.

The window shattered into a thousand pieces, glass fragments of clear crystal and colour rained down on the city square below. Tortured screams of fear echoed off the white stone walls as Millewa plunged towards the ground.

She fell as Wozil once did, fast and hard and hurtling toward the ground.

Panic stricken and weak, Millewa's arms flailed and waved, trying anything to help break her fall. From the immense height she could see her friends, standing beneath the window.

Sydare was running around gathering materials to help break the fall, Phlox was pushing wizards back to try and clear a space and Bee was screaming in heaving sobs as she watched Millewa plummet.

Think.

Her mind was clicking into gear, she had no time to waste. Millewa mustered all the energy she had left, straightened her limbs and willed her being to fly, to be safe.

Within an instant, her descent to the ground was slowed. Millewa could feel the wind beneath her arms, tickling her belly as she glided towards the ground.

She took in her surroundings and swept her way down, thinking of the fire she had possessed only ten minutes prior, she was now controlling the wind. How could this be? Elves only produced and aligned with one element, not two.

Her thoughts were cut short as she dropped on the ground with a resounding thud.

"What happened up there?" Sydare grabbed Millewa by the shoulders, looking her over for any signs of hurt.

"We heard a crash," Phlox added

"And yelling," said Bee, "Plus not to mention the sparks that were spitting out from the roof and walls."

"Are you okay? What happened?" Sydare repeated. Millewa

simply turned to the window, multiple storeys up from where she fell, an elf sized hole now placed in the middle of the glass.

There he was, Finfudune, in the light, standing exactly where she had jumped from, bearing down on them with malicious intent.

"Not now." Millewa held her gaze firm with The King "We have to run."

Millewa was thankful for the tour she had received from The King the day prior. It was proving helpful as they navigated their way around the city, dodging flashes of light and streams of colour that seemed to be increasing with every step.

Millewa led the pack, Sydare hot on her heels and Phlox and Bee's wings fiercely humming as they flew to keep up.

Their lungs were burning and their feet aching, both Sydare and Millewa kicking off their wizard clad shoes to run bare foot.

They could see the golden gate, the arching entry way that would lead them out of the city and back along the track.

Only a few feet away, Millewa was already sizing it up in order to climb over the top, or would she be better to attempt through the bars? Within an instant, their clear view to the trail outside, was gone.

A bone coloured stone wall now stood between them and freedom.

Millewa turned to face her friends, their faces struck with fear and pale with illness. They had to find another way out before it was too late.

"Quick, this way." Millewa ran past them all, heading to the West of the city where the children had played and houses were placed.

They could scale the buildings and jump from their roofs to the wall and over the other side. Yes, that would work.

Head strong and determined, Millewa sprinted past the bakery and ice cream shop, bee lining for the West Side Village.

Horror hit her in the face, another stone wall had been erected. She turned slowly, all around them stone walls were springing up from the ground, distorting the town map and where things were placed.

Beneath their feet the cobblestone path disintegrated into the ground, leaving no trail or path out. Vines grew thick and fast along the newly constructed walls and began whipping them all, stretching and twisting to try and grab a hold of their limbs.

They had to keep moving or the vines and ivy would eat them alive. A clear road up ahead, Millewa ran straight towards it.

"Did I see you glide before," Sydare panted as he sprinted to Millewa and kept her pace. Her days of running from bullies came in handy and she harboured impressive stamina.

"Yeah I did," Millewa replied, "I don't know how it happened, it was out of nowhere. I sort of willed it and it just happened."

"That's awesome, at least we know your element is wind," Sydare smiled and they dodged to the left avoiding a vine as thick as a tree.

“The weirdest thing though, when I was in Finfudune’s office and was supremely mad at him,” Millewa blushed “I made fire sprout from my hands, burning a hole in his chest. My whole body was overcome by heat and it was a tunnel of fire heading straight for him.”

“Wow. You must have two elements then, fire and wind” Sydare looked jealous and a bit hurt.

“Is that rare?” Millewa asked. Another dodge to the left to avoid the poison ivy creating a canopy above their heads, hissing at their heels as they ran.

“Super rare.” Sydare said “Watch out!” A mammoth stone wall came crashing to the ground in front of them, vines and ivy looping through the wreckage to try and get a hand on them.

Millewa felt her back become hot and realised the city guards were right behind them, wands at the ready and firing spells of grey and lilac. A hole had burned through Millewa’s shirt and was now singeing her skin.

She called for the others and tumbled towards the top of the wreckage, there had to be a way out somewhere.

Millewa fell, scraping her knees and hands on the sharp edge rocks, slicing her hand as blood pooled in the crevices below.

“Go ahead.” Millewa rasped, a vine now had a hold of her ankle. She had slowed down her friends enough, they needed to get to safety before the guards caught up.

“I’m not leaving you” Sydare knelt beside her, trying with everything he had to cut through the vine. All his tools and magic weren't working and he looked at Millewa with crying eyes. "I – I can't cut it."

"It's okay," Millewa's eyes were burning, tears streaming down her face. "Just go, it's okay."

"I can't cut it," Sydare repeated, his mouth open and eyes full of dread and sorrow.

"Move." Bee appeared from behind Sydare's head. "Of course you can't cut it, you're an elf. Bosmerch's anti charms work against you. He forgets sprites and the powers we possess."

Bee focussed on her hands, specifically her right pointer finger and Millewa could now see why.

A needle thin nail grew rapidly, as if a splinter was protruding from her nail bed. The guards were ten metres away now.

"Hurry" Sydare pleaded.

"Yes, yes" Bee plunged her needle into the thickest part of the vine, green goo pulsing from her fingers end.

The vines whined and screeched as poison flooded their insides, their green, textured skins turning brown and withered. Bee slipped a hand beneath the vine and Millewa and it crumpled into dust.

Bee retracted her finger nail and shot up into the sky, wings beating ferociously. "We have to move."

An onslaught of spells threatened to be their undoing, every colour of the rainbow attempting to disarm them, mere metres away.

Sydare, Bee and Millewa scrambled up the crumbled stone

and hurtled themselves to the other side.

In front of their eyes a large, grey door stood, with a handle and no lock chamber.

Sydare looked to Millewa and nodded. It was their best hope.

The four of them ran at the door with all the force they had. Tumbling through easily and hitting a cold, wet floor.

The room was pitch black and damp.

They felt around for one another and cuddle in as the darkness around them began to whisper.

Chapter Nineteen
A Promise of Freedom

There was nothing but black that surrounded them. Ongoing, pure darkness filled the room, they weren't sure where it started and where it ended.

Sydare fumbled around for the door in which they fell through, but to no avail. It was gone. Millewa kept her breathing steady, willing her eyes to adjust so she could make out figures at least.

Wherever they were, it was safe, away from the rain of spells and curses they'd just survived. Whispers oozed from the walls, a constant drip tapping away in the background.

Silence.

Dread.

And the smell of decay.

Millewa clasped her hands together, trying to conjure flames to give them some light to work with. She concentrated hard, feeling all the anger she'd felt before The King.

A small ember appeared at her finger tips, glowing like a

blazing sunset, she blew onto her finger waiting for it to spark. A flame, only a minor one now burned at the end of her fingers, like each digit was a tiny candle that had just been lit.

Millewa looked for her friends, Sydare was cold and shivering and Bee and Phlox hadn't let go of one another since tumbling into the chamber.

The chamber in which they stood was a wide open expanse of nothingness. Dark, grimy stone walls encased them in a square set room that seemed to stretch on forever, the same coating the floor.

Pillars of onyx held the room together and glittered with the light from Millewa's hands. Millewa spotted candle burners lining the walls of the room, she didn't want to exhaust herself too much by using her powers and so she lit a burner on her left.

The whole room erupted in light as every candle was lit, crackling and spitting as flames collided with damp drips. Millewa looked ahead, trying to see where the room ended, but it was an everlasting darkness that consumed her from head to toe.

She was thankful she found fire.

"That gate should've led outside Clara," Sydare finally said, breaking the sound of dripping and whispers. "That gate looked like one of the sprite slave gates, the ones they use to access the outer grounds."

"It seems more like a trick to lead us back into Clara," Phlox snorted.

"He's not wrong you know," a new voice called from the

shadows.

Each of them jumped and squealed and looked towards where it had come from. "It is a door us sprites use to get to the outer grounds, but it's also bewitched to lead to our living quarters."

Lantana, the young sprite who served The King directly stepped out from behind a pillar. Her face covered in dirt and slime, her tattered clothes damp as she shivered to talk.

"Lantana? What are you doing down here?" Bee looked positively shocked and rather upset as she took in Lantana and the condition she was in.

"We live here, deep beneath the city." Lantana said plainly, "Whenever our shift is over, we enter through the door and are subjected to the filth of under the city. I was whisked down here the minute you jumped out that window, Millewa. Little did The King know, I heard everything you said and I want to be your insider on this quest."

"This quest is done, Lantana" Millewa sighed. "He is too powerful, too strong. It was a stupid idea."

"War wasn't won in a day," Lantana smiled sweetly at her. "Let me help you, we'll rally troops. We can work together and..."

"And what?" A new voice. A high pitched rasping came from deep in the dark.

They'd never heard this voice before, judging from Lantana's face, it was one to be feared. "You wouldn't be planning treason now would you dear? The King prizes you amongst all the sprites, that is why you do not work in fields and slave about like the rest of them. You are special."

"No sir, I would never. I best be getting back; The King will be expecting me." Lantana gave a grave look to Millewa, her face sullen with regret.

She turned her back and walked to the shadows, Millewa noticing a hollow gap in her back where her wings once were.

No sooner was Lantana gone that another figure emerged. A tall, lanky wizard with brown robes.

His teeth dull and yellow, chipped at the ends with food stuck all through them. He was balding, a thin wisp of brown hair combed over the top. Thick, bushy sideburns lined his face, his blue, bloodshot eyes looked at them fiercely.

"Well, well, well. It seems you have fallen straight into my trap." His yellow grin spread wide across his face. "I knew the minute I saw you run towards that door what I needed to do. A positively grand enchantment. Well done me."

"Who are you?" Millewa studied his face, she hadn't seen him around the city and knew she'd remember a face as strikingly ugly as his.

"Dear Millewa, I am The King's advisor. Rothesay Dig is my name." Millewa imagined his breath was the reason it smelt like decay down there.

"You can't keep us here," Sydare shouted, his energy had obviously been built up from a day of frightful activities, "Come on, we're just kids!"

"Yeah, we just want to go home," whimpered Bee.

"No I don't think that's true at all," Rothesay spat. "The King saw it clearly in that girl's eyes, she's up to something. Planning a revolt. We knew her no good father and she isn't going to stop until she gets what she wants. The King saw flame behind your eyes girly, the burn that only arises during intense rebellion. He's only ever seen that power once in his one hundred and twenty-year life span."

"Damn right I'm up to something," Millewa stood as tall as she could. Narrowing her eyes at Rothesay in disgust.

"Millewa, don't," Sydare gave her a worrying look.

"No. It's not right! Look at Lantana and how filthy she was down here, cold and shivering and oppressed." Millewa's face ran red hot and she felt flames tickling her finger tips. "Why should we stand back while there is such injustice taking place in these lands?

"For centuries, all of Apricus lived in peace and harmony, Finfudune has ruined that completely. Who protects them? Who protects us?"

"King Bosmerch is an incredible leader who serves this land well." Rothesay's eyes gleamed. "You will do well to remember that he is the one who protects you, should you obey his command."

"Millewa just stop. It's gone too far, the best we can do now is to apologise and move on," Sydare pushed.

"Move on? How can I move on when wings are being clipped,

lands are being ploughed by slavery and we live in fear every day? I've seen a whole world since leaving Dewdrop and it's a world I wish to roam freely and explore at my leisure, without fear of being eaten by an Amarok, or ripped apart by a Kobold."

Crackling fire spat from her finger tips, there had to be another way. Millewa sighed, looking around for any route out of the chamber.

Phlox and Bee, she realised, had disappeared whilst she was talking, only the buzz of their wings could be heard. A whisper in her ear confirmed her thoughts.

"Shhh, act natural and keep talking, we have a plan," Millewa shuddered as Bee talked closely and quietly into her ear. "Sprites can eliminate colour at their will and we become invisible in light and dark. Our wings are what give us away. You distract that oaf and leave it to us."

Millewa's gaze returned solely to Rothesay and his yellowed mouth, black rot tearing at the edges of his mouth. Filthy, vile creature, she thought.

"There must be some sort of agreement we can come to sir," Millewa pleaded.

"The King is a forgiving man my child, but you can only push him so far before his kindness is turned to revolt. Your little stunt today proved that you are a danger to this city and this land," Rothesay spat as he spoke. "The only option now is for you to die. If only Sydare here hadn't captured you from your human squander, you may have lived a little longer."

Millewa looked to where Rothesay stood, his feet narrowing together as if they were glued.

A slight flutter filled the silence and Millewa continued to talk as she watched intently at his feet. Rothesay's legs were now being pulled together, did he not feel it? Not notice the pull that dragged his knees together?

Rothesay talked back to Millewa, although she didn't take in a word of what he was saying, mesmerised by the invisible ties that now restricted his movements. Sprites at work, *deadly clever* she remembers Sydare telling her on her first day in Dewdrop Springs.

"*NOW!*" Bee boomed as both sprites sprang back to visibility, their colour strong and vibrant against the harsh darkness.

Positioned on either side of Rothesay's head, their devilish grins spoke volumes about what they were planning to do.

"Hey, what are you..." Rothesay attempted to yell, to scream and to get away. Alas his feet were strung together.

Phlox and Bee in unison took a flying run up and smacked themselves squarely into Rothesay's ears. Dizzied and confused, Rothesay stepped forward, lunging toward Millewa with hands outstretched, trying to grab her, to harm her.

He stumbled, realising the problem that came with his feet and he fell. Face first onto the cool, slippery, hardened floor, echoing a resounding crack as his face connected with the stone.

Sydare, Millewa, Phlox and Bee stared at the thin frame that lay motionless on the floor.

"Is he dead?" Sydare questioned, starting to kick Rothesay's sides with his bare feet.

"No," Bee said flatly. "Stop kicking him like that, we need to leave before he becomes conscious again."

"Guys, we have to go," Phlox urged. "It isn't safe and I can hear the walls beginning to whisper again."

Millewa tore her gaze from Rothesay, looking around the endless chamber for any sign of an exit.

There wasn't one.

Millewa grabbed Sydare's hand and quickly walked towards the far side, the side that was endless and ongoing, the side that harboured immense, menacing darkness. Millewa's quickened stride rapidly increased to a run, sprite wings fluttering swiftly at her side.

Wherever they were under the city, there had to be a way out.

The smell of dead grew and stung their nostrils as if they were travelling directly to the pit of a monster. Dampness was all around them and the candle lights flickered to a dull glow.

"This is useless," Millewa cried out, looking to Sydare with hopelessness stretched across her weary face.

"It's not," Sydare smiled. "Remember my dad's map? The one you risked your life to get back from the Kobold?"

"Of course I remember that, it was only yesterday," Millewa's patience was short and she wished Sydare would just get to the point.

"Well then I'd say you remember *why* it is so important,"

Sydare's grin grew even larger and Millewa felt uneasy at his pleasure. "No matter where you are, or how lost you might think you are, the map will lead you where you need to go."

Millewa's grin now matched Sydare's and she felt an overwhelming sense of relief wash over her like a waterfall in Summer.

She reached into Sydare's pockets and pulled the map from within, she hadn't wanted to bring it into Clara, but Sydare insisted as a precaution. She was really glad he'd snuck it in.

"I slept with it under my pillow," Sydare laughed. "I knew Finfudune would take our clothes and replace them, I didn't want to risk him taking the map too."

"Brilliant," Millewa replied. "So how does it work?"

Sydare unfurled the map, opening it to its full size which mirrored that of an A1 size piece of paper, it was huge.

His hands shaking uncontrollably, Millewa grasped the other side and helped Sydare steady the map. Phlox and Bee took adjacent sides and looked on with concerned faces.

"You point to the part of the map you wish to go," Sydare said finally as he looked up at Millewa. "And… well, I'll let the map show you the rest."

Sydare placed a single finger on the labelled locality *Dewdrop Springs* instructing the map to take him there.

A whirl of light rippled through the chamber walls, electrifying energy pulsating from the maps edges. Sydare looked to Millewa with great delight.

"Good to know dad didn't provide me with a dud," Sydare chuckled. "Let's see where it takes us."

A light shot from the side of the map, creating a pearly white stream in front of them that seemed to go on forever. Millewa could feel the tug of the map, willing them to move with the light source, pulling them towards their freedom.

They wasted no time in watching and ushered Sydare to lead the way, following in fast succession behind him as he navigated through the icy bowels beneath the castle.

The chamber was enormous and daunting, every wall looked the same, every turn opened up to more slimy stone and rats that crept along the walls. The cold was relentless as it bit at their noses and cheeks, Millewa cursing the fact she wore a skirt and short sleeve shirt, goose bumps rising all over her body, she shivered as they ran deeper underground.

Candles were brought to life wherever they ran and were promptly extinguished after they had passed, as if the chamber walls knew they needed to be concealed.

Further and further they ran, waning from exhaustion, hoping soon to see the end of this endless nightmare.

There it was.

A door, not dissimilar to the one they had entered earlier, small and dark at the end of the passage. The maps light plunging through the centre, the exit to who knew where.

At least they might finally experience some day light. A few metres more and they would be to the door.

Without warning or command, the door flew open, casting light into every shadow of the chamber.

Blinded by the setting sun, Millewa winced as her eyes readjusted to outside. She turned, daring to look back at the horrors that stood within the death chamber they'd escaped.

She did not see any monsters or evil creatures lurking behind her, instead an army of sprite slaves that had followed them all the way to the end.

The whispers they'd heard had come from them, hiding behind pillars, ensuring they stayed safe. Their innocent faces shrouded in soot and grime, clothes torn and filthy.

"Come with us," Millewa panted, stretching her arm to the sprite nearest. "Please, this is your chance to be free."

"Freedom will come to us, because we have you Millewa," a young male sprite said. Millewa smiled and made to grab his hand. "But it will not be today."

A frown teared at Millewa's face. Of course they couldn't leave with her today, if they did, they'd all be dead by tomorrow. Millewa instead shook the young sprites hand.

"I will fight for you," Millewa wept. "And I will come back for you."

The sun was setting in the distance and soon the night sky would provide them with cover. The four of them climbed up the stone steps and met the dewy grass just outside the chamber door.

The air was cooling and the afternoon was still and eerie. Without warning the heavy door slammed behind them, once again leaving the sprites in the dark.

Millewa's heart twinged with pain and she remembered her promise to them, that she would return and save them. Sydare stepped forward, gathering his surroundings, staring at the map for guidance when he realised where the chamber corridors had led them.

For there was not sweeping plains or city walls surrounding them, instead a huge, towering rock stood in their path.

Four backpacks concealed between the cavern they'd emerged and the rock face itself. Millewa started to laugh, a raucous, belly laugh that had a stitch prickling her ribs.

Sydare followed suit and howled with laughter. Phlox and Bee stared at one another, smiles splitting across their faces. They had travelled so far underground, all the way to the edge of Clara where they'd hidden their backpacks from The King.

Breathless, tired and heaving gulps of air, Millewa fell to the ground and perched herself against the rock, feelings its cool surface against her sweaty, heated skin.

She had discovered her powers, she had fought off the most powerful being in the lands and she'd run miles underground to arrive where she stood nearly two days earlier.

Her eye lids heavy and weary, she closed her eyes and took deep, resounding breaths. Rest, she *really* needed to rest.

"Millewa, Millewa!" Phlox was pinching her arms trying to get her to wake. "You have to get up, now's not the time to sleep."

Millewa rolled and stretched, had she really fallen asleep sitting up? She looked at Phlox through glazed eyes, refocussing and attempting to wake fully.

"We can't stay behind this rock forever," Phlox's voice was more urgent now. "The guards will be out looking for us soon and we need to get back to Dewdrop Springs."

"We also need to rest," Millewa snapped at him. "Can't you see we are all exhausted? We have been non-stop all day. Not to mention extreme exertion of powers."

"Do you not realise what today meant?" Phlox spat, no humour or kindness in his voice. "We started a war today. A real, scary, blood shed type war. Don't you think it's in our best interests to get back to Dewdrop and warn everyone? The King is furious and wants your head thrown to the dogs. It would be common courtesy to rush back."

Millewa knew he was right, she had no way of arguing. Alvie had warned her what might happen and her worst case scenario had come true. Her actions now put everyone in danger and she had no plan whatsoever on how to fix it.

She looked to the sky and asked her dad for help, willing some of his fight and power to be passed on to her.

Without a second thought, Millewa picked up her bag and snatched the map from Sydare. Light pulsing and leading as she pressed a finger to Dewdrop Springs.

She didn't feel like talking anymore, and so she walked.

Chapter Twenty

An Aisle of Flames

It didn't take long for darkness to incarcerate them. The sun dipped below the mountains almost immediately after Millewa grabbed the map from Sydare. Their only light source being the one that emanated from the maps beam.

Millewa walked like a zombie, feet dragging and trudging across the harsh terrain. She had found it beautiful on the way here, revelling in everything she saw. Now she wished it would all disappear and allow her to move swiftly to sleep.

They walked for hours without speaking, all relishing in the silence and thinking independently about what to do. Millewa detoured from the maps glow, veering off to a familiar patch they had stopped at on the way.

A cool, dampness washed over her as she entered the fruit and vegetable garden. Not like the cold, wet dungeon they'd escaped from. No, this feeling was much more serene.

Trying not to take too long, Millewa grabbed handfuls of berries and stuffed them in her bag, then picked some cucumber and ear shaped vegetable that she didn't know the name of.

A grumble from the bottom bank told her the Kobold was still housed in the cave. She hastened herself and re-joined the group.

"Here," Sydare broke the hours of silence by handing Millewa a brown coloured ball. "Drink this."

"What?" Millewa stared at it, it looked revolting and she wasn't sure she really wanted to drink it at all.

"Just trust me, okay," Sydare was tired and irritable. Millewa had preferred when he wasn't speaking to her.

She obliged his request and popped the brownish ball into her mouth. A swirl of sensation ensnared her senses.

Creamy, rich, full flavoured elements coated her tongue and mouth. It was like all her favourite chocolate bars crammed into one. What shocked her the most was the feeling that came with having it.

Millewa was suddenly wide awake, her eyes bright and alert and ready to walk all night if she had to. Her bad mood was gone and her headache cleared, she looked to Sydare who was just drinking his.

His face washed over with pure joy and calm.

"Ah," he said. "That is so much better."

"What was that?" Millewa twirled in a circle dancing herself around Sydare and the sprites.

"It's a coffee bobble," Sydare smiled. "They are an insane energy booster and their flavour adjusts to whatever the drinker feels like eating or drinking. So for me, it was a lemon and lime cheese puff. Instantly it helps your mood and allows you to carry on for hours more."

"That's incredible." Millewa was baffled by the things they had here, the access and creativity towards every day human items were astounding.

She wondered if that was what coffee tasted like.

The air was serene and the night sky inky and dotted with bright shining stars. A cloudless night guided them back home. Even though there was no light or warmth, Millewa felt safe walking through the night, despite the howls and snarls that could be heard on a flutter of wind.

The journey was long and tiresome, only made bearable by the coffee bobbles that Sydare had in continuous supply. Millewa continued trekking, occasionally stopping for a water or snack break but constantly moving, no matter what.

"We're about halfway," Sydare yawned. "I think we should stop and rest, even if it's for a few hours, we can't keep drinking the bobbles like this, it's not healthy."

The sun was peaking over the mountains behind them, a chilled wind tickling their backs as daylight broke across the lands.

The open expanse around them became visible and Millewa could finally see the stream that had journeyed with them from Clara. A single tree lay to their right, standing tall and alone in the flat scenery that surrounded them.

They looked to one another with tired eyes, shrugging. This

was where Sydare had fought off the Amarok a few days prior, Millewa wanted to go further, she didn't want to stop so close to where it happened.

But alas, her words failed her and she plodded behind her friends who stalked their way to the tree.

The tree was further from the stream than she'd remembered, its thick set trunk wide and inviting, roots bulged from the ground and knotted in clumps around the base.

Millewa was grateful for the rest as she set down some blankets and pillow poppers and propped herself in an elf sized knot.

It didn't take long for her fatigue to take over and sleep consumed her wholly. The breeze flying about her hair, picking up strands and having them dance along the wind. The sun fully up and kissing her cheeks.

She was completely content.

Millewa dreamed of white stone walls and cobblestone paths, of large ice creams and lemon scented breezes. She was utterly happy and relaxed as she flitted through the streets in her white gowns. Her eyes closed and taking in the full heat of the sun.

Her eyes opened and she wasn't in the cobblestone city of Clara, but rather in a foul smelling cavern. Dirt and grime lathered the hard stone floor and snarls echoed from the shadows surrounding her.

She had to run, but her legs weren't quick enough, the Kobold and Amarok closing in on her, their hot breath sticky against her neck. She screamed for help but no one was coming.

The jaws of the Amarok open and gaping as The King cackled in the background ordering the dog to kill.

Sydare was standing over Millewa, eyes wild with worry, scanning over her.

"Millewa," Sydare whispered, she blinked slowly, allowing herself to come back to reality. It was just a dream, she told herself, those things didn't happen. Except they did.

The sky was covered in cloud and rain drops dotted her face, waking her up instantly from her trance.

"Are you alright? You were screaming like mad," Phlox buzzed around her head, making sure she wasn't hurt.

"I'm fine," Millewa blushed, wondering what her physical being was doing while her mind had her stuck in the chamber. "Just a bad dream."

Millewa slung her backpack over her arm, stretching out as she prepared again to walk. Sydare was tracking the sun, trying to see what time they might arrive back.

Bee and Phlox were back near the stream, filling the water bottles for the rest of the journey.

"It's about noon," Sydare looked to the sky, tracing the sun and horizon with his fingers. "We slept far too long."

"We'll make it before dark though, won't we?" Millewa questioned.

"I think so," Sydare pondered. "You gonna tell me what that nightmare was about?"

Millewa could see Sydare studying her face from the corner of his eye, trying not to look directly at her or to pry too much. She shuffled her feet along the ground and told him what happened, from the streets to the chamber and the sickly feeling that accompanied her.

Sydare listened intently and continued looking at the sky.

"It never goes away you know," he added to her story as she finished. "I mean, not really. Not fully."

Millewa turned to face him, a puzzled look on her face.

"What I mean is, I know what it's like to be involved in gruesome, awful things and," Sydare paused and scratched the back of his long, dark curled hair. "It's just I get it. I know what you're feeling and just know you're not alone. The nightmares fade eventually if you're lucky."

"Thanks, for everything, you've really saved my butt these past few days," Millewa gave Sydare's arm a friendly punch and made to walk towards the stream.

"We've saved each other's butts," Sydare grinned and followed her toward the sprites.

The day dragged on and Millewa wondered if they would ever reach Dewdrop Springs. Her feet aching and arms slumped, she wished there were more magic for transportation.

She was just about to ask for another break when the smell of sweet, fresh strawberries wafted in their direction. She would recognise that smell no matter where she was. There was only one place on earth that smelt so delightful and it was Dewdrop

Springs.

The scene was picture perfect, a warm afternoon with a soft, subtle wind. The smell of strawberry drifting in the flurry of air, a sunset as vivid as a burnt orange sky that smouldered brightly in the western plain of the Springs.

"How beautiful," Bee did gymnastics in the air, flipping and fluttering as her wings glittered in the setting sun. "From all that madness we've just endured, this, *this* makes it almost worth it."

"It sure is a sight isn't it, I've never seen anything like it," Phlox beamed at her.

They meandered closer, taking in their home ahead. Millewa staring intently to the lands ahead.

"What a warm afternoon!" Sydare clapped Millewa on the shoulder as he strode toward the entry path. "The warmth, the sunset, it's a perfect gift to come home to."

"I don't think that's a sunset," Millewa's heart sank as she stopped dead in her tracks.

They drew closer to the opening, a wave of heat striking them in the face, the smell of ash overpowering the once sweet smell of fruit.

Charred sprites were flying from the tops of trees and screeches could be heard from within.

Millewa looked to Sydare as Phlox and Bee looked at one another.

"This is all our fault." Millewa's eyes stung with tears.

Dewdrop Springs was perishing under a raging fortress of

flames.

Chapter Twenty-One

Aftermath

Millewa, Sydare, Phlox and Bee drew closer to the edge of Dewdrop Springs, their faces red with the heat radiating from the centre. There was no sign of life and Millewa began to worry the whole of the town had been wiped out, aside from the screams they could hear emanating.

"We should walk closer to the river, they likely evacuated to be near water," Sydare's face was strained with pain, his ears drooped low and sagging.

This was his home that was soon to be piles of ash.

"I'm so-" Millewa began to apologise.

"Don't," Sydare cut her off, he gave her a stern look and began to lead them around the outskirts towards the river they'd frequented before leaving for Clara.

Dewdrop Springs was not too big and it only took them ten minutes to reach the other side of its border.

Smoke and cloud shrouded the area and made it difficult for them to navigate. Sydare led them through his instincts and knowledge alone, passing the battle clearing and through the cover of trees.

The air was clearer in the safety of the trees, clearly undamaged by the fire burning through the town and tree houses. The sun had been setting quickly and beneath the trees a cool, damp air provided much needed relief from the scorching heat.

Millewa grabbed Sydare's outstretched hand and followed him blindly through the thicket of bushes and branches. It reminded her of the first time Sydare had brought her to this world, the scratchy twigs and thick moss underfoot.

She soaked in the moments of silence and peace before the chaos of the river side overtook it. The flutter of Phlox and Bee's wings the only break in the otherwise silent forest.

Millewa could see the end of the trees only a few metres away, leading to the smoke filled, ash ridden air.

The whole town was engulfed in a sea of crimson.

Chaos ensued and elves were working madly to try and contain the flames. Rumbling balls of fire launched from every angle, ensuring every edge of Dewdrop Springs was dripping in red hot flames.

The smell of ash pungent against their noses, the heat stinging at their bared skin. The straggled screams of sprites overshadowing the loud roar of falling trees and houses.

It was a nightmare, and they were all currently living it.

Millewa looked to Sydare, who had tears in his eyes, and grabbed his hand. She didn't know what else to do and felt utterly responsible for what was taking place.

Sprites and elves were working together to try and contain the flames and lessen the damage of what had already disappeared in ruin.

Elves with connection to water were closest to the danger, sweating profusely and helping wipe one another's brows. Their hands were outstretched and solid as streaming jets of water pulsed and doused the base of the flames, extinguishing it for only a moment before a new spark set alight.

Magic flames, Millewa realised. Fire element elves were working with wind elements, attempting to contain the spread of fire, twisting and turning around one another, in tandem splitting and shrinking balls of fire. Flames contorting against their will as if they were being swallowed and spat back out.

Millewa watched on in horror as a wind elf got too close and was swept into the burning mass and was singed with a wavering scream, only surviving due to the water sprites constant jet of moisture.

"What can we do?" Millewa looked pleadingly at Sydare, there had to be some way they could help.

"How well do you think you can harness your powers? We don't need you spreading more flames with your wind and fire," Sydare's words stung like venom and Millewa knew he wasn't happy with her.

Millewa had to take caution when she called on her power. Sydare was right, they didn't need her making things worse but from what she could see, the city was in ruins and nothing more could go wrong.

Elves and sprites were collapsing from exhaustion and heat stroke around them, dropping like flies and falling from great heights. There were only a handful left standing that were sending continuous streams of water to the centre of town, where the monument continued to stand tall.

Sydare's house was the only tree within hundreds of metres left, its thick, strong trunk towering over the river of coal.

Millewa gazed toward it, her eyes wide and calculating. She had borrowed the history book from the library, the book that told her in depth, the history of what happened all those years ago. Along with photos of her parents, of which she had no other copies.

Millewa's heart raced, if the house wasn't burning, no smoke billowing from its windows, maybe she could get inside and grab the book.

It was a huge risk, and a stupid one at that. But what other choice did she have? That book held the key to ousting King Finfudune, liberating her parents, as well as photographic evidence and sentimental value.

Before Millewa had a chance to finish that final thought, her legs were propelling her towards the burning mass.

Sydare screamed for her to step back.

She felt the slight tugs from Phlox and Bee, pulling at her shirt to retreat.

There was no stopping her now, she had this feeling, a strong feeling that she needed that book to continue on. The eagle pin in her pocket buzzed as if to agree with what she was about to do.

Danger loomed around her and she held her breath as the smoke wafted towards her face.

In and out of the house, that's all she needed to do.

Millewa didn't feel the lava that oozed beneath her feet. She moved swiftly and quickly, her eyes set upon Sydare's house, untouched and glowing from the embers that surrounded it.

Alvie's vegetables smouldered, the sweet smell of fruit intensified by the heat, an almost sickly smell that left an unusual tang. She watched as the berry bushes crackled and danced as flames licked at the edges of the neighbouring bush.

Fruit tree trunks littered the path way, splintered wood jutting at every angle, providing obstacles for Millewa to dodge.

She tiptoed her way over countless squished squashes and ducked beneath low lying branches, hoping for her life they didn't snap and crush her.

The door to the house was hanging by a hinge, swaying with the force of the wind sprites magic, creaking slowly and eerily in the midst of the fury.

Millewa pulled the door back with a staggering heave, lifting the door completely off. She discarded it to the side and looked up the echoing void that led to the living quarters.

The pulley system would be useless, the rope burned and singed. Millewa would have to climb the winding staircase all the way to the top.

With a great sigh she took the first step, from an already exhaustive day, this was the last thing she wanted to be doing. The eagle pin she held in her hand, buzzed with enthusiasm as if to egg her on to continue.

She raced up the stairs as fast as she could, her breath sharp with quick intakes, the smoke and incline burning her lungs. Millewa felt as if she couldn't breathe, uneven and shaky, she fell into the house from the final steps, collapsing onto the hardwood floor in a crumpling heap.

"That had better be my useless son coming to save me," a straggled voice called from the hall. Millewa looked up, eyes dazed and stinging. Ella Jones.

"No ma'am, it's Millewa," she spluttered in reply, attempting to get to her feet with immense difficulty, pushing from the floor onto her hands, then her knees.

"*You* again?" Ella yelled. "What are *you* doing in my house? Get out you filthy vermin and tell my no good son or grandson to retrieve my head."

Millewa crouched, trying to keep low from the hazy air that filled the ceiling. She crawled her way to the hall entry and made her way slowly to her bedroom.

Ella yelled profanities at her the whole way down, screeching for Alvie or Sydare, her head cup boiling over in rage.

Millewa avoided her gaze and slipped into her room.

The large window lay open to the outside, the screams of

elves and sprites echoing from below. The river lay not far from Sydare's house and Millewa could feel the panic pulsating through the citizens of Dewdrop, and herself.

The room was littered with charred leaves, some still glowing at the edges with a red glaze. Millewa stared at her once beautiful sanctuary, one of green walls and darkened wood accents, soft furnishings and fluffy bed sheets. One where she would sit on the window sill reading and drawing, taking in the lemon scented breeze that danced across the stream below, one where sleep came easily and her dreams were filled with wonder.

Now, what stood before her was a derelict room covered in black and darkness. The eeriness made Millewa shudder and she walked to her bed and grabbed the huge history book from underneath it.

She raced her way from the house, running from Ella's severed head and trotting down the winding staircase to the burning ground below.

Millewa gasped at the bottom, taking in as much fresh air as she could before ducking through the garden's side gate. She was only a metre through the Jones' garden when a booming crack thundered across the land, reverberating across the river and into the mountains.

Without a minute to think, Millewa watched as Sydare's tree house began to sway, and crack, and sway, until finally a resounding snap bellowed and the ground shook with impressive force.

Sydare's house had shattered to the ground and burst into fiery flames. Nothing in Dewdrop Springs was safe anymore.

Millewa slowly backed away, turning only when she could hear Phlox and Bee squealing that she had returned alive and well.

"We thought you were dead!" Bee cuddled the side of Millewa's face as she sidled up to them both.

"What *were* you thinking?" Phlox added, rolling his eyes.

"I was thinking," Millewa started, "that to defeat The King and prove he is the most evil being in this land, I needed this."

Millewa held out the book to show Phlox and Bee, both of them gaping at the book, then back to Millewa.

"Where did you find this?" Phlox spluttered.

"I was given it by the town librarian, he said it may come in handy," Millewa shrugged.

"He wasn't wrong," Bee added. "This book not only tells the history of Apricus in the perspective of elves, but it is one of the only history books in modern times that hasn't been tampered by The King's magic to nullify and distort what really happened all those years ago."

Millewa stuffed the book into her already full backpack, trying to stay calm and unsuspicious, if any King lovers caught wind of what she possessed, things could be much worse for her.

Millewa could see Sydare, leaning against a small tree by the riverbed, staring unblinkingly at his fallen home. The final nail in the burning coffin. Millewa walked to him and put her arms around him, knowing that nothing could replace the feeling of losing his childhood home, but she had nothing to say.

"It's everything I've ever known, this place," Sydare's voice choked as he tried to hold back his tears.

"What happens now?" Millewa asked.

"I – I don't even know. This isn't a very common occurrence," Sydare said with a bit of anger, as if this whole ordeal was Millewa's fault.

He had offered to help her and she thought he was being a bit unforgiving of what had happened, but she tried to keep an open mind.

Around them, sprites and elves continued to work, salvaging what they could from the burning mass and wreckage.

To Millewa it seemed pointless, the town was in absolute ruin. A mass of soaked charcoal and slow burning coals, there was no way to repair it.

Millewa watched as elves and sprites retreated, cuddling one another and watching the ever burning flames continue to destroy their homes. She looked out for a sign of someone she knew, someone to help comfort Sydare, but alas she saw nothing.

Coughing and spluttering erupted from the centre of the town, a deep, heaving cough that sounded like a very sick elf. Millewa looked towards the clearing where she exited Sydare's yard, a stout figure making their way through the smog.

Heavy, slow steps and a dark silhouette against the scarlet sky, carrying something rather large under their arms. Millewa readied herself in case her powers would be needed in combat.

The figure drew closer and Millewa's heart beat faster, thumping in her chest like a drum. Her hands raised and ready, she took a tentative step forward, wind beginning to swirl from her fingertips, she didn't want to risk the use of flame in case the blame was cast upon her.

The stocky figure stepped in the clear and light of the riverbed's edge. Ashen faced, panting and bleary eyed, Alvie walked towards Millewa, his mother's head resting in the crook of his arm.

He looked beaten, unhappy and utterly upset. His eyes directly focussed on Millewa, bee lining right for her.

"What happened Alvie?" Millewa broke the silence between them. The air as thick as custard, his eyes piercing through her. She felt uneasy and prepared to cower and wallow in his disappointment.

"The King is what happened," Alvie retorted, he then rounded on Sydare, completely ignoring Millewa's guilt stricken face. "What in the world of all that is good happened out there?"

"Dad, I…" Sydare began to stutter, tears streaking his face once more.

"Don't Dad me," Alvie's words were as cold as ice, disgust painting his face as he looked down his nose at them both. "I told you what would happen, I warned you before you left."

"I know, I really thought we had a handle on it," Sydare looked up, he had been staring at his feet since Alvie walked over. “The King was waiting and prepared, as if a trap had been laid.”

“And you thought, the best option was to push forward, not to retreat?” Alvie’s eyes were unwavering and strong, Millewa felt uncomfortable at the seriousness he emitted. “The Amarok should have been enough warning for you, enough to turn you around.”

Behind Alvie, another building fell crashing powerfully into the earth and shuddering the dirt beneath their feet.

Trees were crumbling and snapping, no sign of life coming from where there was once a lively, positive town.

“How did you know about the Amarok?” Millewa cut in, they hadn’t spoken to anyone about the creatures they’d encountered, there was no way for Alvie to know.

“I am the leader of Dewdrop Springs you foolish girl,” Alvie spat at Millewa and she instantly regretted her decision to say anything at all. “I know every creature Finfudune controls and where exactly they are placed within the lands. If *you* hadn’t been so hasty to go and ruin everything with your bright ideas, I would have been able to help you in that regard. You chose unwisely and now you need to live with the consequence.”

Sydare looked sheepishly at Millewa and back to his father, his cheeks rosy with embarrassment and shame. Behind them, the town continued to smoulder and burn.

Millewa looked around at the river’s edge, sprites and elves already making shelters and temporary camps. She saw the librarian, Hillard conjuring mounds of earth and dirt, constructing makeshift mud huts, others using leaves to weave rooves.

Children were cuddled to their mothers whilst they tended to fruit they managed to salvage from the wreck. The sun had fully set and they were plunged into darkness, only the moonlight glistening off the water provided light.

The river water pooled and swirled, bioluminescent fish swam lazily around the banks. Millewa turned back to Alvie, a grave look across her delicate face.

“I only tried to fight for our freedom, to allow us to live according to how we want to,” Millewa said.

“Not only did you fight for our freedom,” Alvie looked at her with sadness. “You started a war.”

Millewa looked around her at the damage that had been caused in just a few hours and she realised, this was a war they likely could not win.

Chapter Twenty-Two

A New Home

Mornings in Dewdrop Springs were always a pleasant occurrence of chirping birds, rustling leaves and the happy elves and sprites greeting one another good morning.

The morning after the burning was far less cheerful and rather more sombre. The sunrise was bleak and underwhelming, a dull orange peaking from over the hills, only further highlighting the damage that had been caused.

An earnest apricot glow across the stark contrast of blackened soot. It was obvious now that everything that had ever been in Dewdrop Springs was now decimated.

No more soda stops or outdoors shopping, no seed packets that would burn her hands or walks through the vegetable patch eating as she gathered the salad ingredients for Berrima.

There was a giant black hole where her home once stood, *her* home. It is what Dewdrop had become to her in a short couple of months and she longed for the time she had before pursuing The King and elven salvation.

Millewa stretched out in her tent, the one they had stayed in whilst journeying to Clara. This time, only Phlox and Bee kept her company. After the events of last night and her run in with Alvie, Sydare was quite short and distant with her, he had sauntered off with Alvie to their tent on the opposite side of the river and she hadn't seen him since.

"It feels weird, doesn't it?" Bee turned in her bed to face Millewa, propping her small head upon her hands, staring intently. "Like as if we're still out on our adventure, camping for fun, not out of necessity from a burnt home."

Millewa stared back blankly at Bee, she had no words for what had happened and every time she tried, she began to cry. She appreciated Bee and Phlox staying with her, she really didn't have anyone else.

"Thanks," she added blandly.

"Don't sweat it," Phlox leant over the top bunk to cast a gaze at Millewa. "My house by the river was being used as a refuge for mothers and babies last night, I'm more grateful for you in this moment than you are for me."

"We're practically family ourselves after all we've been through, don't think you're getting rid of us that easily!" Bee chuckled.

"Old grumpy pants and his sidekick will come around too," Phlox said mockingly, acting like Alvie and stomping about the room.

Millewa was appreciative for their humour and kindness and

even fashioned a smile herself.

"I hope I'm sidekick and not grumpy pants," Millewa jumped, the voice from the tent entryway startling her.

Sydare stood, slumped and sheepish looking towards his friends. "I'm sorry, Millewa. I shouldn't have been so hasty to judge or believe it was all your fault. We were in it together and I see that now."

"As Bee said," Millewa grinned, "We're practically family after what we've done. Come here!"

The four of them hugged for a long time, enjoying one another's presence and love. No matter what happened, they were here for each other.

Millewa smiled and breathed a sigh of relief. She was home.

"Dad wants to see you," Sydare blurted out quickly after their hug exchange.

"He does?" Millewa instantly felt queasy, she didn't want to see Alvie after the events from the night prior. "He's not going to yell at me again is he?"

"I mean, Dad is an old grump so I can't make any promises," Sydare winked. "I'll come with you anyhow."

Millewa brushed her teeth and chugged some water before following Sydare outside. The river was flowing swiftly, a slight mist playing atop the water's surface.

Young elves were playing merrily by the stream, making mud pies and hurling them at their siblings.

Sydare steered Millewa away from the cheerfulness and

towards what she dreaded most. Seeing what was once Dewdrop Springs in the daylight. It was something of nightmares.

Where Millewa once saw colour and light was now black and death, the lingering smell of ash and fire stinging her nostrils.

Amongst the heaps of coals, right in the dead centre of town where her father's monument was, stood Alvie in robes as black as the trees around him as if he was mourning.

Sydare took Millewa's hand and led her towards his father.

"Good morning to you both," Alvie said with depressing sombreness.

"Good morning Alvie," a quiet and scared reply from Millewa.

"It is truly a town of ruin now isn't it," Alvie sounded more light-hearted now, as if he was attempting to make amends.

"How long will it take to rebuild?" Millewa prompted, hoping this was the beginning of a relationship renewal.

"Oh dear Millewa," Alvie smiled. "We are so fortunate with magic; it will take no time at all. The King could've wiped us out completely if he really wanted to, but that's not what this attack was about. No one died yesterday, thank the stars, because Finfudune had sent a beam from Clara, alerting us to the impending danger.

"He warned us the town would be set alight and gave us plenty of time to get out and save ourselves. He was sending a message by burning us to the ground, he never intended to kill or injure anyone. He is merciful like that."

Millewa looked around at the dishevelled elves and sprites wiping soot from one another and cleaning their filthy clothes in the river. She thought about The King's warning and wondered why Alvie hadn't saved his mother's head sooner, instead leaving it until the tree was about to fall.

"Is there anything I can do to help?" She asked.

"The King, my dear child, is forgiving. I'm afraid you will need to just lay low and ride out the storm. He's certainly been triggered by your whole charade and we need to be careful now with how we act around him." Alvie's face was soft and gentle, how she imagined her own father would've been in a situation like this.

Millewa walked herself around the river to a quiet bank past an outcrop of trees that hadn't been torched. It was now mid-morning and the sun was relentlessly beating down upon her.

The summer holidays in the human world would've surely started and she sighed at the thought of lake swimming and outdoor campfires in the backyard. How did it come to this?

She slipped her feet into the water and flicked her toes about in the shallows, watching tiny fish approach and scatter as soon as she made a sudden movement. She sat for a while, thinking and contemplating what she needed to do.

Millewa had really been enjoying her life in Dewdrop Springs and believed this is where she truly belonged. A thought that continually crossed her mind as she replayed Alvie's words in her head, was maybe she was better off leaving altogether.

Ridding them of her and letting them start fresh and new without the burden of her presence. But where would she go? The human world was always a possibility, but she had seen how Stella and John had reacted when she'd gone missing, they were overjoyed.

She wouldn't survive out in the wilderness of Apricus, so that wasn't an option. She turned the eagle pin in her fingers.

"What should I do?" she asked the pin, as if it would have some magical answer.

Nothing.

It had always buzzed with excitement when facing potential dangers. Why could it not help her now.

"Should I go back to the human world?" she pressed on.

Nothing.

"Should I stay here?" she tried again.

Nothing.

"Should I stay here? And fight?" A pulse rippled through her body, as if every nerve inside her was electrified.

Her fingertips and toes were beaming and charged with energy. She knew this pin was special and she wasn't entirely sure how, but her gut said to trust it and to stay and fight for what she believes in. Freedom from oppression and the slavery of elves and sprites.

She clasped the pin to her chest and rose from the bank of the river, Millewa needed to tell Sydare of her plan.

She dusted her legs and turned on her feet, heading back to the makeshift campsite. Loud, bellowing horns and trumpets beckoned in the distance, short repeated bursts echoed through the forest.

Millewa knew the tune and her stomach turned. The King was arriving in Dewdrop Springs.

"My dear council of Dewdrop Springs," Millewa could hear Finfudune's voice booming through the open clearing of decay. "It is a terrible tragedy that has occurred on your land, we must be thankful that no lives were lost during this time.

"However, you see, this was a necessary reminder that things as they are is how it is supposed to be, your service to the kingdom and greater region of Apricus is duly appreciated.

"In saying that, if beings beneath the power of Clara decide it suits them to challenge that authority, my next cascade of flame may not be forewarned or as forgiving. Please take this warning now, with care.

"My visit is not only of sombre opinions, but one of great sacrifice. The rebuilding of Dewdrop Springs is vital to the survival of Clara, the elf and sprite contributions to the kingdom are greatly needed and Claran wizards are already feeling the effects. I offer mine and my council's services to rebuild the town on the western side of the river, where no trees have been maimed and flat ground lays beyond. Please don't dilly dally and assist in the great rebuild of Dewdrop Springs."

Cheers erupted from the elves and sprites, tears of joy streamed down their faces as they hugged one another in sure solidarity. The King beamed down at all of them from his podium, his white teeth gleaming in the daze of the sunlight.

Millewa shuddered at the whole affair. There was no doubt in it, Finfudune was a wordsmith and a true politician. He knew how to win over the crowd whilst still sending ruthless jabs of warning at them. Millewa could read between the lines and knew his talk was directed solely at her.

Her heart burned with fire and she could feel her fingertips getting hot. *Cool it.* She thought to herself, *now is not the time.*

Millewa straightened her clothes and joined the throng of elves and sprites barrelling to the other side of the river, across a stable wooden bridge fashioned by The King with only a flick of his wand.

They wasted no time in recreating Dewdrop Springs on the opposing side of the river. Every elf and sprite was put to work, no one was to sit out unless they were sick, injured or had children. There were no other exceptions.

Alvie led the charge in determining where houses would be built. Sourcing the biggest and thickest trees for elves and smaller, thick branched trees for sprites. He of course chose the largest, most robust tree for his own home, enlisting wood dwelling sprites to hollow it out.

Earth elves helped clear the land, removing unnecessary trees and bushes, making way for pavers and buildings. Alvie used his own skills as an earth elf to clear and tunnel soil in the front of his yard, Millewa could only assume this is for his abundant vegetable patch. She figured he'd be really impressed by the one she'd found by the Kobold cave.

Water sprites constructed their homes from mud piles, whist fire elves used their flames to hard set the huts.

Wind elves shook the neighbouring trees to drop leaves and bark for furnishings.

Finfudune spent most of his time displaying his wand work and making furniture for every single home.

Mother sprites and elves spent the day hunting and gathering food, preparing it for what seemed to be a huge feast.

By the end of the day, an amazing amount of progress had been made and every being sat down as one in the what would be the centre of town, thick cobblestone pavers (similar to those in Clara) were laid and blankets were strewn for comfort.

Rich stews, mashed potatoes and baskets of fruit were littered across the town circle and the smell of fresh bread tickled their nostrils, wafting from nearby ovens.

Millewa looked around at what had been built and was in awe of how much they'd achieved.

Every elf and sprite had a tree house or mud hut in progress, marked by fire blazes with their initials. The town square was now a circle and pavers had been set. Shopfronts had been marked and new trees erected to suit the needs of each shop.

There was still a long way to go, but by golly was it a good start.

Millewa sat with Sydare, Phlox and Bee for dinner, laughing

and giggling about the day's events. Sydare had stubbed his toe on an upturned root and Phlox had laughed so hard water spurted out his nose. The four of them found it so funny, they kept retelling it over dinner and ending up in stitches all over again.

Millewa could feel eyes watching her throughout the whole ordeal, burning into her like the blazes in the surrounding trees.

She turned her head slowly towards the river, where she felt the light coloured eyes stinging into her. Finfudune stood by the edge of the water, eyes boring into her head.

She rose from where she was eating and walked slowly towards him.

"You've done a really great thing here today," Millewa said as she approached the water, standing next to The King, he was much taller than she remembered from a few days ago.

"My people need to be safe, they cannot live in tents forever, it would be counterproductive," he spat back with slight venom, The King turned to face Millewa.

"I was wrong," Millewa looked into those pale light eyes. "We really do need you and your people, *I* am really grateful for everything you've sacrificed."

The King's white teeth gleamed as he looked at her, smiling a broad, winning smile.

"I am glad you now see it that way. As I said to you in my office, we can all live harmoniously as long as you believe *and* behave."

"Undoubtedly, I believe you should be in power and I would

like to stay here if you'll allow it? The human world was once my home but I believe I'm safer in your world than it." Millewa felt bile rising from the pit of her stomach, the words tasting like dirt as they left her mouth, a filthy, gritty taste of lies and deception.

She was playing with fire, but at least she knew now how to control it.

"I am more than over the moon to hear you say that young Millewa, of course you may stay," The King was now positively beaming at her, he believed every word she said. "I feel in time we can have a really wonderful friendship!"

The King turned on his heel, almost skipping back to camp. He headed to his makeshift quarters and disappeared for the night.

Millewa stayed by the river, watching the moon's reflection in the water.

"That was a really nice thing you did," Millewa jumped as Sydare, for the second time that day, scared her as he walked from behind a lone tree. "It was a smart thing to do, apologising I mean. Now we can just live like elven kids do and not worry about the rest of it."

"Are you serious?" Millewa had a tone of annoyance in her voice. "I was obviously not serious, that whole act about him being great was fake. I'll bide my time, once this all blows over we'll strike again. That man is evil and I'll be damned if I let him rule my life."

"Millewa that's dangerous, you see what happened here."

Sydare shuddered as if reliving the whole ordeal all over again.

"Next time we just need to be more careful, more strategic," Millewa grinned. "The only way this ends, is with that dictator dead."

"I don't know Millewa…" Phlox and Bee flew up to them as Sydare looked worriedly at Millewa.

"I'll go with or without you, Sydare." Millewa said with a shrug.

"We're with you!" Phlox and Bee said in unison.

"Oh how could I let you all go without me," Sydare put his arm around Millewa, Phlox and Bee resting on their shoulders. "I'm with you all until the end."

Millewa hugged her friends closely and felt their warmth against her. She stared to the inky sky and watched as a shooting star cascaded across the jet black of night.

There was no doubt in her mind, that she was exactly where she needed to be.

Made in the USA
Las Vegas, NV
03 February 2025

17517395R00134